THE WICKER MAN

'On the first of May the Beltane fires would be kindled,' said Darryl. 'And human and animal sacrifices would be burned in the fire.'

'You mean burned dead?' said Frankie.

'Oh yes,' he said softly. 'Burned very dead. The best sacrifice of all was thought to be a boy or a girl captured from a neighbouring tribe. They'd probably have been about your age.' Darryl's sharp, bird-bright eyes fixed on the four of them. 'You see, they believed they had to placate the forces of nature and that human sacrifices were absolutely vital for their survival.'

'So, how long ago did all this stop?' asked Frankie.

'Did I say it had stopped?' said Darryl.

Books available in the DARK PATHS series

DARK PATHS

The Wicker Man

Allan Frewin Jones

MACMILLAN CHILDREN'S BOOKS

Created by
Allan Frewin Jones and Lesley Pollinger

Thanks to
Leigh Pollinger and Rob Rudderham

First published 1998 by Macmillan Children's Books
a division of Macmillan Publishers Limited
25 Eccleston Place, London SW1W 9NF
and Basingstoke

Associated companies throughout the world

ISBN 0 330 36806 0

3 5 7 9 8 6 4

A CIP catalogue record for this book is available from
the British Library.

Phototypeset by Intype London Ltd

Printed and bound in Great Britain by Mackays of Chatham plc, Kent

Contents

CHAPTER ONE
The Old Dark House

'He lives here?' Regan Vanderlinden's voice rose in astonishment as she stared up at the semi-derelict old house that reared over them. 'Darryl Pepper lives *here*?' She shook her head. 'I guess the stories about him having gone crazy must be true. A person would have to be totally insane to live in a spook-factory like this.'

'This is the address Mrs Tinker gave me,' Frankie Fitzgerald said uncertainly. She shoved a hank of thick golden hair off her face and looked up at the narrow, dingy top-floor windows of the neglected Victorian house. She pointed skyward. 'Up there, apparently. Top flat.' She took out her notebook and opened it, holding it in front of Jack Christmas' eyes. 'See?'

'Top Flat. Twenty-three Herne Road,' Jack read. He nodded. The number 23 was scrawled in white paint on a cement pillar half-hidden by a rampant privet hedge.

Beyond the hedge lay a rough area of dirt and gravel. The house itself stood alone, well back off the road. In years past, this solitary aloofness must have given it an air of grandeur, but now it just looked ashamed of itself; dilapidated and furtive.

Blank windows stared emptily at them. Paint peeled into tattered fronds. Tall trees leaned inward towards the house, as if to cover its embarrassment with a lattice-work of branches.

To one side, a rusty old van slumped in the shade of the trees like a dead elephant.

'It's spooky to the *max*,' Regan declared, her American accent ringing out loudly in the quiet of the bright Surrey afternoon. 'It's like some kind of reject from an Addams Family movie.' She looked at Frankie. 'Are you sure this was such a good idea? What if the guy really is insane, like people say?'

Frankie shook her head. 'I don't believe any of that stuff at all. He's probably just gone a bit . . . um . . . eccentric. People do if they spend a lot of time on their own – but I don't imagine he sleeps hanging upside down from a rafter or flies about on a broomstick.' She laughed. 'Not in broad daylight, anyway.'

'That does it,' said Regan, with a toss of her long hair. 'I'm out of here.'

'Don't be daft,' said Frankie. 'He'll be OK. Honestly.'

Tom Christmas looked at his older brother. They both had the same mop of light brown hair and the same deep brown eyes, but Jack was paler and quieter than his inquisitive younger brother. 'What do you think?' asked Tom. 'Are you getting any weird feelings about this place?'

Jack shook his head.

Regan looked sharply at the brothers. 'Why did you ask him that?' she said to Tom.

'Well, sometimes—' Tom began.

'No reason at all,' Jack broke in. 'Are we going to do what we came here to do, or are we going to stand here nattering all afternoon?'

'Let's go for it,' said Frankie. She marched out ahead of her three companions, her feet crunching on the gravel as she strode determinedly towards the ominous black front door under its shadowed gothic porch.

Regan eyed Jack and Tom thoughtfully as they trooped after Frankie. There was something a little kooky about those two. Well, not so much Tom, who seemed like a regular 12-year-old boy (i.e. crazy), but his 13-year-old brother, Jack, with those wide-spaced faraway eyes – there was certainly something odd about him. She'd thought it from the first moment the two of them had walked into that lunch-time ACE meeting at school a couple of weeks back.

New boys in the school. New kids on the block. Regan knew all about how that felt. Her feet had hardly touched ground for five minutes at a time since she'd been born in the family mansion in Westchester, in upstate New York.

Over the eleven frantic, helter-skelter years of her life, Regan had lived in Beijing, Sydney, Lagos, Moscow – you name it, her parents had dragged her there and dumped her there, in a succession of huge houses filled with furniture they didn't own and teeming with servants and secretaries and personal assistants and officials who acted like Regan was invisible.

And now her mother's high-flying diplomatic work had brought her to the American Embassy in England, where she hobnobbed with statesmen and royalty. And for once in her life, Regan found herself living in a place she really wanted to be.

3

She liked the little old town of Lychford. Maybe this time she'd have the chance of forging some *lasting* friendships. She felt like she'd made a good start with Frankie and the boys – even though sometimes a look in Jack's eyes would send ice-water down her spine: like he was seeing stuff that regular people never saw.

Regan shook her head to clear her thoughts as Frankie stepped up into the porch of the grim old house. Under the shade of the tall gothic arch, the air was still and cool. The shadows cast by the fierce spring sun seemed cut out of black card, so sharp they might draw blood.

Frankie pressed the bellpush and waited for something to happen. Frankie was thirteen – the same age as Jack, but unlike the Christmas family, who had only been in Lychford for a few weeks, she'd lived there all her life. That was how come she knew Darryl Pepper. He'd been a student at St Columb's School a few years ago and, up to last summer, he had occasionally come back to give the most amazing talks at the lunchtime meetings of the ACE club: the school archaeology club.

But Darryl Pepper's talks had started to get a bit wild. He began to suggest that some of the strange old myths and legends they were studying might be true. The club was run by a teacher who didn't think much of ideas like that; Mrs Tinker was very much into provable *facts*. Darryl stopped being invited to talk at the lunchtime meetings. Rumour had it that he'd gone barking mad. Potty Pepper, people called him. Frankie didn't believe he was really insane – just a bit *different*. At least, she hoped that was the case.

It was on behalf of the ACE club that Frankie

4

and her friends were calling on Darryl Pepper that afternoon. They needed some expert information, and, mad or not, Darryl Pepper was exactly the right person to ask.

If he ever answered the door.

'There's no one in,' said Tom. 'Let's go.'

'Someone's coming,' said Jack.

'I don't hear anything,' said Regan, listening with her head against the door panels.

The door opened so suddenly that Regan almost landed ear-first in the hall. A small, wrinkled face peered up at them from unexpectedly close to the floor. It was a little old lady, no more than four feet tall. She looked like an old-fashioned doll that had been in the bottom of someone's wardrobe for too long.

'Not today, thank you,' she piped.

'No! Wait!' Frankie said quickly. The little woman was already closing the door. 'We've come to see Darryl.'

'Ohhh, no, no, no, no, no,' shrilled the old lady, shaking her little wizened head until her wispy grey hair flew. 'Darryl doesn't like *people*. Darryl doesn't see *people*.' She managed to make the word *people* sound deeply unpleasant – as if she was talking about a disease.

'But we're *nice* people,' said Regan. 'He's expecting us. He'll want to see us – guaranteed!' She stepped over the threshold into the large, gloomy hall. 'Hey, this is some kind of place you have here. My name's Regan Vanderlinden.' She thrust out a hand and the startled little woman took it gingerly. Having parents that she only saw once or twice a week had given Regan bucket-loads of self-confidence.

5

'Well, I don't quite know if . . .' The little old lady seemed totally disarmed by Regan's attack. 'But if you . . . I suppose . . .'

'These are my friends,' Regan charged on. 'Frankie Fitzgerald, and Tom and Jack Christmas. Jack's the lanky one with the blank expression. Is Darryl in? He talks about you all the time. He says you're the coolest landlady in the entire world.' Regan grinned. 'And I bet he's right, too!'

'He's in,' said the old lady, watching with baffled eyes as the four young people entered her hallway. 'Of course he's in. He's always in. I suppose if he's expecting you . . . you'd better go on up. His is the last room you'll get to – right at the top. Under the eaves.'

'Thanks,' said Regan. 'Come on guys, we're late as it is – get with it!'

Tom looked around as they mounted the stairs. The place seemed to have been done out in early teapot-interior: in oppressive shades of brown. He could just make out the shapes of monstrous brown flowers under the dingy varnish that coated the wall-paper. The sort of flowers that, if he had Jack's imagination, would come alive and swell and burst out from the walls to engulf him in a deadly, sickly embrace.

'Regan, you are such a storyteller!' hissed Frankie as they climbed the stairs. Darryl wasn't expecting them at all. 'And what makes you think she's the landlady?'

'There's only one bell,' said Regan as she ascended into the stale-smelling brown old heart of the house. 'Old lady. Old house. Two and two makes four. No problem.'

'Are you always like this?' asked Jack.

Regan glanced down at him as she rounded the banister and started up the next flight of stairs. 'Like what?'

'Like a bulldozer.'

Regan grinned. 'Yeah, pretty much all the time. Why? You got a problem with that?'

'No, I just wondered,' sighed Jack. If Regan had been a musical instrument, she'd have been a bugle. It was exciting to be with her, but rather exhausting, too – like being caught up in the slipstream of a tornado.

'One day you'll really come unstuck,' Tom said hopefully. He thought the brash American girl needed taking down a peg or two: she was far too pushy and in-your-face.

'Yeah, sure!'

They came to a second landing. Doors and corridors led off. All brown. All coated in the deepest of glooms; steeped in age-old silences. Another flight led upwards.

'Top flat,' said Frankie, looking up.

'Yeah,' said Regan. 'The *belfry*. Let's hope there aren't any bats.' She grinned down. 'You scared of bats, Tom?'

'Nope.'

'Sure?' Regan's voice was full of laughter. 'They can get tangled in your hair, you know.'

'Yes, I'm sure,' said Tom, glaring up at her. He really wished she didn't get such a kick out of teasing him. He was a whole year older than her – he ought to be able to keep up with her, but she always seemed to have one more wisecrack up her sleeve. It could be infuriating.

They came to another landing. A narrow staircase led up to a single door under the sloped eaves of

7

the roof. Sad light filtered down through a grimy skylight. A bare forty-watt bulb fought weakly to disperse the brown darkness.

'I think we've hit pay-dirt,' said Regan. She stepped aside. 'You wanna go first, Frankie?'

'Why?'

'You know the guy,' said Regan. 'He might freak if he sees a strange face peering in at him.'

'Strange face,' chuckled Tom. 'You can say that again!'

'I meant a *stranger*'s face,' said Regan.

Frankie mounted the final long thin flight of stairs. The carpet was threadbare. The treads were painted brown and thick with dust. The huge, ugly brown wallpaper flowers stared over her shoulder as she neared the closed door.

On the top tread was a pile of unopened mail.

'What are you waiting for?' whispered Regan from a couple of treads down. 'Make like a woodpecker. Rat-tat-tat!'

Frankie raised her arm, her fingers curled into a fist. There was something in the atmosphere of the old house, something that made her wary and uneasy; a watchfulness that oozed out of the walls and made the hairs stand up all along her arms.

What if Darryl Pepper really had gone mad?

She was about to knock when the door sprang open from the inside.

She saw a looming shadow. Before she could react there came a yell which startled her witless and almost sent her tumbling backwards down the stairs.

CHAPTER TWO

Darryl Pepper's Attic

'Who on earth are you people? What are you doing here? What's going on?' The figure at the head of the stairs stepped forwards into the dim light, revealing itself to be, if not exactly *ordinary*, at least *human*.

Frankie was clinging on to the banisters with Regan right behind her. The two brothers were halfway up the stairs – their ears still ringing from the cry of alarm that the man had let out when he had opened the door to find Frankie standing there with her fist in the air.

Darryl Pepper may not have gone completely crazy, but he certainly looked a little eccentric – especially for someone who was only in his late teens. He was as thin as a stork and dressed in baggy grey trousers and a frayed shirt, over which hung a shapeless green cardigan with low-hung, bulging pockets. A narrow tie dangled from his collar. Above his stork-thin neck was a face that seemed to want to peck at you. Heavy, horn-rimmed glasses perched on his long beak of a nose. Brown hair that was so pale that it almost looked grey, stuck up in uncombed spikes all over his head.

'Whoo-hooo-wheee!' gasped Frankie as she regained her balance on the narrow stairway. 'You took me by surprise there!'

'Who are you? What do you want?'

Frankie took a deep breath. 'I'm Frankie Fitzgerald. Don't you remember me? From the archaeology club at school – from the ACE club? We met a couple of times when you came to give those talks.'

Darryl Pepper leaned forwards and peered at her. 'Yes. I remember you. You asked intelligent questions. You had long blonde hair.'

Frankie blinked at him. 'Er, yes, I still do,' she said uneasily.

'Yes. Absolutely.' He stared at the three others in turn. 'I don't remember any of you.' His eyes fixed on Regan. 'Black hair and blue eyes. That's an unusual combination. You must have Celtic roots.' He switched his gaze back to Frankie. 'Why are you here?'

Frankie quickly introduced the others. 'The thing is,' she continued, 'Mrs Tinker has set us a project.'

'We need a whole heap of information about May Day festivals,' said Regan. 'Mrs Tinker said you were the guy to talk to. She said what you don't know about May Day festivals could be written on the head of a pin with a spray-can.'

Frankie glanced down at her. 'That's not *exactly* how she put it.'

'I don't do talks any more,' said Darryl.

There was a brief, awkward silence.

Regan pushed up past Frankie. 'So? May Day festivals? Have we come to the right guy, or what?'

'You'd better come in.' He looked anxiously at the two boys. 'All of you, I suppose. Don't touch anything.'

The enormous room was brighter than the hallway, but not by much. It was oddly shaped and the ceiling sloped in under the roof. The entire room was cluttered with an incredible assortment of things: old newspapers and magazines, bits and pieces of junk and machinery, a half-finished matchstick model of a cathedral, and another of an ocean liner. Things that looked like bizarre abandoned experiments, and a whole array of instruments and tools and bric-a-brac.

Even Regan was rendered temporarily speechless.

Darryl led them to a solitary window set in an alcove. A computer stood on an old wooden desk, bathed in a pool of bright afternoon sunlight. The walls were covered in cork tiles, upon which were pinned a multitude of scraps of paper and pages torn from magazines.

The computer screen was full of writing and the desk was scattered with open books and notepads.

'Wow!' said Regan under her breath. 'Unreal.'

'Have we disturbed you?' Frankie asked. 'It looks like you were in the middle of something really important.'

Darryl waved a dismissive arm. 'Just some research. A pet theory of mine on the Great Fire of London. It can wait.' He sat down with his hands between his knees and his bird-like head stretched forwards. He cocked his head and looked at the four of them. Jack noticed a bright gleam in his eyes, as if a private joke was dancing behind his glance.

'So, Beltane festivals, eh?' said Darryl.

'Um, May Day festivals, actually,' said Tom.

'Same thing,' said Darryl. 'The Celtic festival of Beltane took place on the first of May.'

'I knew that,' Tom said quickly. Regan gave him an amused look but didn't say anything.

'But why come to me?' asked Darryl. 'Mrs Tinker knows as much about these things as I do.' He smiled. 'Well . . . *almost* as much.'

'Yes, but she's a teacher,' said Jack. 'You know what teachers are like – they expect you to find things out for yourself.'

'So, you came here to me,' said Darryl, his smile broadening. 'A wise choice.'

'You'll help, then?' said Frankie.

'Absolutely. Where do you want to start?'

'At the beginning,' said Tom with a grin. 'And then carry on until you get to the end.'

Darryl gave him a curious, hawkish look. 'The beginnings of the Beltane rituals go back a very long way,' he said with a sly half-smile. 'Way back in the Iron Age, the Celtic peoples of these islands marked the four significant stations of the year with ancient rituals and sacrifices. *Samhain*, in the depths of winter; *Imbolc*, to herald the approach of spring; *Beltane*, to welcome the summer; and *Lughnasadh*, to celebrate the harvest. And to the Druids the festival that announced the coming of summer was one of the most important. The first of May – Beltane.'

Frankie pulled a slim notebook out of the back pocket of her jeans. 'I'll jot a few things down, if that's OK,' she said. She smiled at Darryl. 'Sorry – carry on. That's exactly the sort of stuff we need.'

'On the first of May the Beltane fires would be kindled,' Darryl continued. 'And in the old days, human and animal sacrifices would be burned in the fire.'

'You mean, burned *dead*?' said Frankie.

Darryl's sharp, bird-bright eyes pinned her to the wall. 'Oh, yes,' he said softly. 'Burned very dead.' He paused for a few seconds to let this sink in.

'The best sacrifice of all was thought to be a boy or a girl captured from a neighbouring tribe.' Darryl's eyes moved from Frankie to Jack. 'They'd probably have been about your age. Their sacrifice would be attended with age-old rituals and celebrations. On the eve of Beltane all fires in the village would be extinguished. Then the needfire – the Beltane fire – would be lit on a hilltop outside the village. There would be feasting and processions, dancing and singing . . . and then the Beltane *carlines* – the sacrificial offerings – would go to the flames.'

'Uh, excuse me,' Regan broke in again. 'Why exactly did these guys think that cooking a kid on May the first was such a totally brilliant idea?'

'To placate the forces of nature,' said a soft voice behind her. She turned to see that faraway look again in Jack's large brown eyes. 'They thought that if they didn't make sacrifices to the spirits of nature, then the summer might never come, and their crops might fail in the autumn. If that happened they'd all die of starvation and cold in the winter.' He gazed at Regan. 'You've got to remember that those people didn't understand how natural things worked. They had no idea why the seasons changed – so they could never be sure that winter would automatically turn into spring, and spring into summer, and so on.'

'So, they gave it a little helping hand,' said Frankie. She looked at Darryl. 'That was it, wasn't it? That was the reason for the sacrifices.'

'Absolutely. The sacrifice would be offered to the spirits of nature and all would be well,' said Darryl.

13

'The days would lengthen and the land would grow warmer and they could look forward to a fine harvest.'

'Yeah, but that's just totally crazy,' said Regan. 'Nobody in their right mind—'

'It's not crazy,' interrupted Darryl. 'If you lived the life of the ancient peoples of these islands, the last thing you'd want to do is upset the forces of nature. They believed that human sacrifices were absolutely vital for their survival.'

'So, how long ago did all this stop?' asked Frankie.

'Did I say it had stopped?' said Darryl.

Frankie gave him an uneasy look, but then she saw the twinkle in his eyes. 'I think people might object to being barbecued on a bonfire these days,' she said. 'At least – I'm sure I would, even if it *was* to make certain that everyone else had a good summer.'

'The sacrifice of human beings stopped . . . oh, around two thousand years ago,' said Darryl. 'But people still have May Day festivals where they build bonfires and burn effigies. But I don't want to make this too easy for you. You people should find some of this out for yourselves. Carol Tinker wouldn't think much of me if I just told you everything.'

'I didn't know you still saw Mrs Tinker,' said Frankie.

'I don't,' said Darryl. 'But we have the occasional chat.' He swung in his chair and pointed to the computer screen. 'E-mails,' he said. 'I can get in contact with people all over the world on this piece of equipment. You'd be amazed how many archaeological websites there are on the Internet. Look, I'll tell you what I'll do. I'll print you out a list of books you can use to find out all about Beltane festivals and rituals. How's that?'

'That would be great,' said Frankie.

Darryl tucked himself up close to the computer and his fingers rattled at high speed over the keyboard. The screen changed and changed until he seemed to find a site or a page that suited him. A few seconds later a sheet of paper was working its way out of his printer.

On it was a long list of books.

'There you go,' he said. 'That lot should keep you busy. You should be able to find most of them in the library. And remember: the only way to absorb knowledge is by rigorous study and hard work.'

'Uh, yeah. Thanks,' said Regan, giving him a peculiar look. 'I'm sure we'll remember that.' She looked at the others. 'Well, guys? How about we get out of Darryl's hair and let him get on with his work.'

'Yes, we should be going,' said Frankie. 'Thanks for all your help, Darryl. Look, I know it's a bit of a cheek, but would it be OK for us to come and see you again if we come across anything we can't make sense of?'

Darryl turned his chair and gave the four of them a long, slow look. 'Yes,' he said at length. 'That would be OK.' He stood up and stalked over to the door.

It was an odd sort of departure for the four friends. They trooped out of the huge old attic room, expecting to be ushered downstairs, but instead Darryl just shut the door on them.

No one spoke until they were out of the weird old house.

'Well,' said Frankie. 'He wasn't so bad, was he?'

'Like you said,' agreed Jack. 'He's just a bit eccentric.' He looked at the list Darryl had printed out. 'He's certainly given us plenty of research material for the project.'

'It'd take months to read all that lot,' said Tom, leaning over his brother's arm, 'even if the library's got the books in the first place. Mrs Tinker wants the project in by the end of next week. That doesn't give us very long.' Mrs Tinker had timed the project so that it coincided with the first of May, which was to fall on the bank holiday Monday of the following week.

'Then we'd better get with it, guys,' said Regan. 'Last one to the library gets ritually sacrificed and burned at the stake!'

'Don't say things like that,' said Jack. 'Not even as a joke.' He looked back at the run-down old house. While Darryl had been speaking of the ritual sacrifice of young people, a horrible feeling of unfocused anxiety had swept over Jack for a few chilling moments.

The horror had passed quickly, but the memory of it left a stain on the bright afternoon, and not for the first time, Jack Christmas vehemently wished he was free of the unsettling burden of his strange family legacy.

CHAPTER THREE
Bodin Summerley

A black night. Ebony hills humping along the horizon, their uneven outlines only discernible because it was there that the acid-white, needle-sharp stars were blotted out. A cold, clammy wind. Sweat chill on the face. Eyes aching, straining for something that would make sense of this horrible place. Low moaning and chattering all around in the pitch blackness.

A thick, acrid smell. Crushed leaves. Sickly sweet flowers. Broken branches. The feeling of being stifled. Something across the face. Covering the head.

And then, infinitely far away and no bigger than a pinpoint, a flame, flickering on a hilltop like a lizard's tongue. And then another lick of flame, as if in answer to the first. And another, and another until every hump of barren earth was crowned with a horn of red fire.

And on the sighing winds that flowed down from the hilltops, Jack could smell the danger.

'Jack? Jack – are you listening to a word I'm saying?' Mrs Christmas finally caught her son's attention. He had been staring out through the kitchen window at the hoary, bent-backed old oak tree that dominated the upper half of their long garden. He had been *seeing* the bleak, barren landscape of his dream. As vivid as the breakfast bar and the bowl of cereal that sat untasted on it in front of him.

He turned to look at his mother. She had her bulging briefcase under her arm and was by the door – ready to climb into the old Morris Minor and head off for her new job at the town library.

'Sorry,' he said. 'What did you say?'

'What time are you expecting to be home from the field trip this afternoon?'

Tom came hurtling into the kitchen and nose-dived into his breakfast, his shirt half-out of his trousers, his hair like an abandoned bird's nest. Upstairs, the new bedroom the brothers were sharing was filled with a faint sulphurous odour where a small early-morning experiment with his chemistry set had gone slightly wrong.

'I'm not sure,' said Jack.

'Mrs Tinker said it'd only take about a quarter of an hour to get there,' mumbled Tom through a mouthful of cereal. 'So even if we stayed there an hour or so, we'd still be back before six. Easy.'

'OK,' said Mrs Christmas. 'Six is fine. Your dad'll be in by then. Get Mrs Tinker to phone if you're going to be much later, right?' Silence. '*Right?*'

'Yes, Mum,' said Jack.

She frowned at him. 'Are you OK?'

'Fine. I had a dream. That's all.'

She looked at him for a moment as if she was debating internally over whether she had the time right then to talk about it. 'It's all the disruption,' she said at length. 'You'll be right as rain once the dust settles.'

'Yeah. I expect so.' Jack glanced at the wall clock. 'You'll be late.'

His mother blew two quick kisses and disappeared.

Seconds later the front door slammed and Jack and Tom were alone in their new home. It was a promotion for Mrs Christmas that had brought the family to Lychford. They had been there three weeks now and everything still seemed new and strange to Jack, although Tom seemed to have adapted within days.

St Columb's school wasn't so bad, as schools went, and the ACE club had been a real find, especially for Jack who loved anything to do with history. Tom had joined up too, not so much because the idea of lunchtime talks on ancient Etruscan pottery thrilled him to the core, but simply because the two of them had always done everything together.

The ACE club proved to be more fascinating than Tom had expected. According to Mrs Tinker, who ran the club single-handedly, the whole area around Lychford was perfect hunting-ground for Iron Age and Bronze Age settlements, Roman towns and temples, Saxon cemeteries and Civil War fortifications. Not to mention the chance of unearthing ritually severed heads and dismembered bodies, bronze axes, Celtic swords, and hoards of ancient jewellery!

And after school today they were set to pile into the school minibus and drive off to the nearby village of Bodin Summerley where a real, live archaeological dig was taking place. Mrs Tinker had been given special permission to take a small group of students there to see the dig in progress.

'So, what sort of dream was it?' Tom asked. 'One of *those*?'

'Sort of. I don't want to talk about it. If I talk about it, it'll make it too real.' Jack frowned at his younger brother. 'I don't want you saying things that make people suspicious. Regan was giving me some very odd looks yesterday. I don't want people to think I'm peculiar.'

Tom chuckled through his breakfast. 'You don't want people to *know* you're peculiar, you mean.'

'This isn't funny.'

'Oh, chill out, Jack, who – ow!' Jack had clamped his hand down hard on Tom's wrist.

His eyes were unusually sharp. 'It isn't funny, Tom. You wouldn't like it. You wouldn't like it at all.'

'OK. OK. I get the message,' said Tom. 'You're Young Mister Normal. And mum is Mrs Normal. And Gran is Granny Normal. We're all totally normal in this family. Everyone's normal. The whole world is normal. Could you let go of my arm before my hand drops off?'

Jack lifted his bowl and slurped back the last puddle of cereal-flavoured milk.

'We'd better go soon, or we'll be late.'

'Yeah. I'm almost ready. Five minutes, *max*.'

Jack grinned. 'Max? That's a Regan word.'

'Get out of here, I've been saying *max* for ages.'

'No, you haven't,' said Jack. 'You've only started using it since you met Regan. You picked it up off her.' Jack grinned broadly. 'And people only pick up words from people they really like.'

Jack slid down off the breakfast stool as Tom shot him a look of pure horror.

'That's not true,' exclaimed Tom. 'She drives me crackers.' He shouted after Jack as he vanished, laughing upstairs to get his school things. 'Regan is the most irritating person in the world! She's big-

20

headed and bossy and annoying to the absolute *ma*—Arrgh!'

A peal of laughter rang down the stairwell.

In the event, they didn't need the school minibus for the ACE field trip. In fact, by the time people had finished dropping out for one reason or another (dentist appointment, detention, football match, too busy, can't-be-bothered-on-a-Friday-afternoon, etc.), from the full ACE membership of twelve, there were only four people left – five including Mrs Tinker.

But Mrs Tinker was used to setbacks. She took it in her stride with only a passing comment about people not taking advantage of one-off opportunities. She abandoned the idea of the minibus, and Frankie, Regan, Jack and Tom climbed into her roomy, rackety Land Rover.

Five minutes later they were out of Lychford and on the road to the little village of Bodin Summerley.

'We went to see Darryl yesterday,' Frankie told Mrs Tinker. Frankie was in the front passenger seat. The other three were in the back.

'Did you now? I hope you didn't just get him to write your project for you. That wasn't the idea at all.' Mrs Tinker glanced at the others in her mirror. Her eyes were bright, sparkling blue behind her big glasses, her page-boy cut blonde hair hanging half over the lenses. She was a small, bubbly, excitable woman who was able to convey her own passion for archaeology to other people by sheer enthusiasm. She reminded Jack of a can of fizzy drink that had been given a good shaking just before being opened.

'Nope, we didn't do that,' said Regan, hanging

over the back seat. 'He didn't tell us much at all. He just gave us a list of books to read.'

'Good for him.'

'He did tell us that the May Day thing started in the Iron Age,' said Tom. 'Mrs Tinker? When exactly was the Iron Age?'

'It lasted from about 700 BC to 43 AD,' said Mrs Tinker.

'Why did it end in 43 AD?' asked Regan.

'Because that was when the Romans invaded Britain,' said Frankie.

'Exactly,' said Mrs Tinker. 'I'm glad Darryl mentioned the Iron Age, because this dig I'm taking you to is possibly from that same period.'

'Have they found anything interesting?' asked Regan.

'We'll see when we get there.'

'They've dug up a sword, I bet,' said Tom. 'A real Iron Age sword.' He looked at Regan. 'For lopping annoying people's heads off. *Swooch! Roll! Thud!*'

'Nah,' said Regan dismissively. 'I bet they've found a pot of gold coins. Treasure trove. We'll all be rich.'

'You already are rich,' said Frankie.

'My folks are,' said Regan. '*I'm* not. My allowance is, like, minuscule!'

'Maybe they've dug up a bronze figurine of one of their gods.' Frankie looked across at Mrs Tinker. 'Is it something like that?'

'The last I heard, nothing had been dug up,' said Mrs Tinker. 'They're still excavating, so far as I know.' She grinned. 'Digging down, yes? I'm not saying any more. Wait and see.'

To a passing motorist, Bodin Summerley was one of those towns that seemed to consist of a few cottages stretched along the grey thread of the road, a row of quaint shops, a church hall, a small garage and a pub. A blink and a sneeze and you'd be through it and out the other side without even noticing that it was there.

But as Mrs Tinker navigated her big car into the cramped space afforded by the pub car park, Jack had the feeling that Bodin Summerley, in one form or another, had existed on that site through a vast stretch of time.

The pub was a big, ramshackle old place with an Elizabethan, wood-and-plaster exterior and small mullioned windows. A sign hung from a roadside post: *The Wicker Man*. The painting on the swinging sign was of a huge wickerwork figure against a blue sky. Dwarfed by the size of the thing, tiny people danced at its feet.

Jack felt drawn to the painting. While Mrs Tinker locked the Land Rover up, he walked over to the signpost and stared up at it.

Some of the little people were playing musical instruments. Others were busy piling faggots of wood around its legs, and from one corner of the heap, a plume of smoke was rising. Jack felt the hair at the nape of his neck prickle.

'Oh, that is so *gross*!' Regan had come up behind him and she had obviously just seen the thing to which Jack's eyes had been irresistibly drawn. 'There are *people* in there!'

A ladder leaned against one of the wicker giant's legs, and a section of the wickerwork was open like a door in the huge thigh. People were crammed inside the frame. Victims. Sacrifices. Scores of them. Now he was this close, Jack could see limbs and faces showing between the wicker stanchions all over the huge construction. Struggling limbs and frightened faces.

'Well,' said Frankie, who had followed to see what was going on. 'At least now we know how they managed the human sacrifices.'

'Not nice,' said Regan. 'Not nice at all.'

'Hey! Are you coming or what?' They turned to see Tom and Mrs Tinker heading around the back of the pub. Tom was yelling and waving.

The three friends pulled themselves away from the gruesome sign and followed the other two.

'Can you imagine what it must have been like to be burned alive?' murmured Frankie. 'It's just so . . .' She shook her head, lost for words. 'All those poor people!'

They rounded the back corner of the pub and came to what once must have been a garden. Benches and wooden tables were piled on one side and, hard up against the back wall of the building, a deep round hole, about three metres in diameter, had been excavated. Earth was piled nearby, smelling strongly: musty and pungent.

The top of a ladder showed. Two young people crouched at the lip of the hole, staring down: a young man and a young woman.

Tom and Mrs Tinker were just behind them, their eyes similarly fixed on the dark throat of the hole. The top of the ladder shifted, as if someone was climbing it. A hard hat rose into sight. Tousled grey hair showed underneath.

'Incredible!' The excited, dirt-smeared face of a man appeared. He was climbing using one hand. 'Fantastic!' Something large and lumpy, like a big, wedge-shaped chunk of brown stone, was cradled in his other arm. 'Luke! Molly! Give me a hand here.'

Luke helped the grey-haired man out while Molly took the thing from the crook of his arm.

Regan pushed past Tom, determined to be the first of the gang to see what all the excitement was about. Molly held the thing across her arms, as carefully as if it was a baby.

As she leaned forwards and finally got a good look at the thing in Molly's arms, Regan let out an exclamation of disgust and dismay. It wasn't an Iron Age sword, nor was it a pot of coins, nor a bronze figure.

Whatever the four friends had been expecting, the lumpy, wedge-shaped thing in Molly's arms was something far stranger and far more disturbing.

CHAPTER FOUR
The Head in the Well

'What on earth *is* that thing?' exclaimed Regan with a shudder.

Up close it no longer looked like stone: it looked like very old leather. Bones protruded in places from the wrinkled shape – white and light brown. The lower jaw was missing, but a few big yellow teeth were still attached to the upper jaw.

'It's a horse's head,' Molly said, her voice cracking with excitement. 'A mummified horse's head.'

'Ew!' Regan backed rapidly away. 'Make some space, guys, I'm gonna pass out! That's gotta be the most hideous thing I've ever seen.'

'They buried a *horse* all the way down there?' asked Tom. He was determined not to be freaked out by the head, despite the evil, broken half-grin of those ugly yellow teeth. 'Why would anyone do that?'

The grey-haired man climbed out of the hole. 'Carol,' he said, smiling at Mrs Tinker. 'Welcome. And you've brought some people. Great.' He flashed a toothy smile at the four friends. 'You couldn't have timed it better. We're just getting down to where the votive offerings were buried. We found the head an hour or so ago. We cleaned it up in position and photographed it. That's always the first thing to do before we move anything.' He patted earth off his clothes and took off his hard hat.

'Frankie, Jack, Tom, Regan – this is Philip Milligan,' said Mrs Tinker. 'He's the man in charge of this dig.' She looked at the ridged and furrowed head. 'It looks like you've been successful, Philip.' She glanced at the four friends. 'Philip and his team are investigating an Iron Age well. It dates from the middle of the first millennium BC. That's right, isn't it, Philip?'

'We think so, yes.'

'Sorry if I'm being thick,' said Frankie, 'but what's a horse's head doing down a well?' She looked at Philip Milligan. 'You mentioned votive offerings. Aren't they, sort of, gifts for the ancient gods? But why would the people mess up their water supply by throwing a horse's head down their well?'

'Excellent question,' said Philip. 'This wouldn't have been the well they used for drawing water. It may have dried up, or become polluted. Or it may not be a real well at all. If my suspicions are correct, this may be a ritual shaft or pit.'

'Cool!' breathed Regan. 'A ritual shaft. Far out!' She frowned at Philip Milligan. 'What exactly is a ritual shaft?' She eyed the grim trophy with deep unease: what if those heavy, wrinkled eyelids suddenly opened and the grotesque thing actually *looked* at her with its ancient, dead eyes?

Philip grinned at her. 'We're not at all sure what the shafts are. Some of them may well have been used as ordinary wells at some time, or as storage pits, but others seem to have had no other function than as holes into which' – he smiled at Frankie – 'gifts to the gods were deposited.'

'The Celtic people had deep-rooted beliefs in the underworld,' said Mrs Tinker. 'Wells and shafts just like this one may have been a link between the Celtic worship of water and springs, and their belief in a supernatural world beneath their feet. They'd throw ritual gifts into the shafts to keep the gods happy and to ensure the fertility of their crops. In some places, hoards of gold and jewellery and silver have been found.'

'I said it would be pots of gold!' said Regan. 'Hand me the spade, Mr Milligan, I'm going prospecting!'

'It's more likely to be other animal deposits,' said Philip. 'Or maybe even *human* relics.'

'Uh . . . scratch that request,' gulped Regan.

Philip Milligan chuckled. 'Molly – hand me the head for a moment, will you?'

He took the fascinating, horrible old horse's head from his assistant. 'Now then, look here,' he said. The others gathered around him, although Regan's face was scrunched up and she only had one eye open – just in case. 'See that indentation in the forehead?' He indicated an area where the curve of the bone high between the eyes was pushed in to form a hollow about the size of a child's fist. 'That was where the creature would have been poleaxed to kill it before the head was cut off and deposited in the well. Interestingly enough, these sorts of rituals could well have taken place around this time of the year.'

'At a Beltane festival, you mean?' Frankie said.

Philip Milligan looked at her in delight. 'Well done, Frankie! I can see you people know your stuff.

Yes, the animal could well have been sacrificed at a Beltane celebration.'

'What's all this?' boomed a hearty voice from behind them. 'Visitors? Sightseers? I'll have to start charging an entrance fee!'

They looked around to see a tall, stocky man whose shirt strained over an enormous belly. He was grinning. He had a round, ruddy face and a nose that looked like a ripe strawberry. A fringe of hair surrounded his big bald head.

'Edgar – this is Carol Tinker,' said Philip. 'I told you she would be coming over with a few students. Carol – everyone – this is Edgar Lovejoy. He owns the land we're digging on.'

'The land and the pub,' boomed Mr Lovejoy jovially. 'It's been in my family for five generations. There've been Lovejoys at The Wicker Man since 1856. And there's been a pub on this site since 1620.' The others cleared a space as he barrelled forwards. He stopped in his tracks, like a galleon taken aback by a sudden squall, and stared at the mummified head with bulging eyes.

'Well I never,' he said. 'What have you got there?'

'It's a horse's head,' Tom said quickly, before Regan got a chance. 'The ancient Celts put things like that down wells to stay friendly with the gods of the underwear . . . um . . . *underworld*, I mean.'

'Gods of the underwear,' giggled Regan. 'Tom, you're a genius!'

Tom glared at her but sensibly kept quiet.

Jack felt a curious prickling between his shoulder-blades – not exactly the feeling of being watched, but more a vague sense of a sudden anger or fear, hot as a desert sun on his back. He turned. A window snapped shut in the side wall of a cottage that over-looked the site.

'This is every field archaeologist's dream come true,' said Philip Milligan. He looked around at the small crowd. 'And it was such a stroke of luck! I just stopped off here for a pint and a ploughman's a few weeks back. Edgar had people in, digging up an area of concrete to expand the lawn. I was sitting out here when I saw them uncover the mouth of the well. I recognized what it was immediately.'

'And I said to myself, Edgar, I said,' broke in the landlord, 'what would pull in the punters even more than good ale and a bigger beer garden? A special attraction, I said to myself. Our very own bit of ancient history on display. I'm thinking of adver-tising. We could get coach parties from as far as . . .' He paused, his eyes fixing on something beyond the small group at the head of the well. 'Hello! Some-one's in a hurry!' He bellowed over their heads. 'What's up, Godfrey? Fear? Fire? Foes? Or have you won the lottery, old boy?'

Every head turned. A low stone wall divided the pub garden from a patch of overgrown land, on the far side of which stood the cottage that had drawn Jack's attention only a short time ago.

A man was running across the wasteland as if rabid dogs were at his heels. He came to the wall and scrambled over it, his face distorted with the effort.

He was a hawk-faced elderly man, frail and wiry, his thin stooped body wrapped in a brown suit. The crumpled jacket billowed out behind him. His white hair streamed. His eyes stared. His paper-thin hand clutched at his chest.

'Godfrey! Godfrey! My dear chap, what on earth is the matter?' said Mr Lovejoy as the breathless old man reached the group. 'You look like you've seen a ghost!'

'What . . . have you . . . found . . . ?' the old man wheezed as he gulped air into his narrow chest.

'Something very exciting indeed, Mr Fox,' said Philip. He smiled. 'I'm afraid you were wrong, you know.' He looked at the others. 'Mr Fox and I had a little wager. He said the well would only turn out to be a couple of hundred years old – but I was sure it was a lot older than that. It was far too near the building for a start.' He smiled at the panting old man. 'Well, you owe me a pint, Mr Fox – the severed horse's head we've just unearthed proves that this is definitely an Iron Age site.' His voice became tinged with anxiety. 'Are you OK, Mr Fox?'

'Iron Age?' gasped the old man. 'Are you sure?'

Philip Milligan nodded. He held out the mummified head. 'I think this confirms it,' he said.

The old man shrank away, staring at the head with wild, almost frightened eyes.

'Put it back,' he hissed. 'Put it back. You don't know what you're doing.'

'Don't worry,' said Philip Milligan, looking slightly puzzled. 'It's perfectly safe.'

The old man licked his lips nervously. 'Safe?' he muttered. 'What do you know about what is safe?' He stared at the horse's head as though the sight of it appalled him. 'If you don't put it back, I won't be responsible for what will have to happen . . . you can't . . . you can't . . . ahhh . . .' His breath wheezed and he stumbled backwards.

Frankie was standing right next to the old man and was just in time to slip a strong hand under his thin arm and prevent him from collapsing onto the earth like a marionette with severed strings.

As Frankie supported him, she was quite surprised to feel steel-hard muscles under the loose material of the sleeve of his jacket. Godfrey Fox might be as thin as a stick insect, but he wasn't quite the enfeebled old gentleman that he looked.

Jack came up and took Mr Fox's other arm, and between them, the two friends helped the old man over to one of the nearby benches. Sweat was pouring down his face. Mr Lovejoy disappeared into the pub.

'I'm so sorry,' mumbled the old man. 'I don't know what . . . ohh . . . this is most embarrassing . . . I seem to have over-exerted myself . . . oh, my . . .'

'Did you see the way the old guy sprinted over here?' Regan whispered to Tom. 'No wonder he's feeling dizzy. I'm surprised he hasn't had a heart attack.'

'Make way! Make way!' Mr Lovejoy came thundering along the garden, brandishing a glass with some amber liquid in it. 'Napoleon brandy,' he said, handing the glass to the old man. 'Nothing like it for dealing with the collywobbles.' He watched solicitously as Mr Fox sipped the thick liquid. 'That's the ticket. You must look after yourself, Godfrey. Really, you must. How would we ever arrange the festival without you? Now then!'

'What festival is that?' asked Jack.

Mr Lovejoy's eyes twinkled. 'We've decided to revive the old May Day festivities. They used to be the biggest event in the region when I was a lad – a real money-spinner – but there hasn't been a May festival in Bodin Summerley for thirty years or more.' He rubbed his hands together. 'Just think of it – all those thirsty tourists flocking to have a gander! It should boost trade no end! The advertising placards are going up today. We're expecting a monster turnout!'

After a few sips of the brandy Mr Fox seemed to have recovered and everyone's attention went back to the marvellous Iron Age find.

'It's getting a little bit too dark to do any more digging this afternoon,' said Philip, looking up at a roll of grey cloud that was creeping in from the west. 'We'd better put a tarpaulin over the well in case it rains overnight.' He gazed down at the mummified head like a proud parent with a newborn infant. 'Luke? Fetch a finds bag, will you? We need to keep it cold and damp until we can examine it properly back at the University.'

'I thought you were intending to spend the night here,' said Mr Lovejoy. 'Surely you don't need to go all the way to the University and back? Couldn't the head be kept at the pub for the night?' His face split with a smile like a slice of melon. 'We could put it on the bar – the punters would be queuing up for a look!'

'Don't take offence, Edgar, but that's the last thing I want,' said Philip. 'We need to keep this find quiet for as long as possible. There are unscrupulous collectors around who'd be only too willing to steal it, given half a chance. I've encountered that sort of thing before.'

'In that case, may I make a suggestion?' said Mr Lovejoy. He cocked his head towards Mr Fox. 'Godfrey could look after it for you.' He spread his hands. 'His house is secure enough, surely? Especially as no one will even know the ... er ... the *find* is there.'

Jack saw Mr Fox flash the landlord a brief look of alarm.

The old man began to speak. 'Edgar, don't you realize the signific—'

'Now, now!' boomed the jovial landlord, silencing Mr Fox with a loud clap of his plump hands. 'Now, then, Godfrey, I know you're still upset about losing your bet with Philip, here, but we mustn't play dog in the manger, eh? We must help the fellow out, Godfrey.' Mr Lovejoy gave the old man a sharp look. 'I think your cottage would be the perfect place to keep the thing. Don't you, Godfrey? Hmm? Don't you?'

The old man's tongue moved drily between his lips. 'Yes,' he said after a few moments. 'Yes. I'm sorry, Edgar. You're quite right.' He looked at Philip Milligan. 'I have an excellent cool cellar. The thing could certainly be kept there overnight. I can guarantee no one will know of it.' A pale smile lifted the corner of his mouth. 'And you can take it away to your University tomorrow – when you have more time.'

Jack had the sudden urge to say *No! Don't do that! That's a really bad idea!* But then the feeling was gone again before he could speak.

Mr Milligan nodded. 'That would be perfect,' he said. 'Molly will carry it over to your cottage. Luke – get the tarpaulin out of the car, will you, please?'

'And I think we'd better be heading back to Lychford,' said Mrs Tinker. She shook hands with Philip Milligan. 'Thanks very much for allowing the children to share such a marvellous moment. I'm sure it's something they'll never forget.'

'My pleasure,' said Philip.

'Come on, you lot, back to the car,' said Mrs Tinker.

Frankie saw Jack watching old Mr Fox and Molly

as they walked back to the cottage beyond the wasteland.

'What's up, Jack?' she asked, puzzled by the intensity of his gaze.

'Oh, nothing.' Jack gave a half-smile. 'Just making sure the old fellow doesn't keel over again.'

'He was in a state for a while,' said Frankie as the two of them walked to join the others at the Land Rover. 'I still can't work out what he got into such a panic about.'

'No,' murmured Jack, looking thoughtfully over his shoulder at the diminishing figures. 'No, neither can I.'

CHAPTER FIVE

The Kindling of the Dream-fires

*T*he blackness of the night was less intense, but just as menacing. The landscape was filled with furtive, flitting half-shapes. Jack felt as if he was drowning in the bitter smell of smashed leaves and bruised flowers. Something plucked at his ankle and a thin, reedy cackle of laughter sounded close to his ear. The swollen hills were closer this time, and the cold red fires larger. Bent figures danced in silhouette across the flames.

Something jabbed into Jack's back, but when he turned to see what had attacked him, he found that he was unable to move. He was encased in something – something that imprisoned him from head to foot, like a coffin of branches and twigs, leaves and flowers. A coffin with eye-slits. A coffin which allowed him a ghastly view.

Distorted, semi-human shapes approached him out of the shadows. Crouching. Evil eyes glinted, reflecting the prancing flames. Teeth snapped. There was more laughter. Then he felt himself lifted by a host of hands and borne up a long slope towards the nearest of the fires. The flames blossomed and cracked, as if the fire was breathing in the sick night air and exhaling it as a feverish, intense heat.

Limbs of flame reached out towards him and the chattering voices lifted in a wild howl of exultation.

Jack awoke in an ocean of sweat. His duvet was tangled around him like a stifling cocoon.

A peevish voice sounded in the darkness. 'Jack, for heaven's sake, shut up, will you.'

The mundane reality of his shared bedroom was like a slap of cool water. He sucked in a shuddering breath. 'Sorry. I was dreaming.'

'Yeah, tell me about it!' moaned Tom. 'You woke me up.'

'Sorry.'

'I'll be glad when Dad finishes decorating my room and I can get some proper sleep for once,' said Tom. 'Without you performing in the middle of the night!'

'I don't do it to annoy you,' said Jack.

'Yeah, well it *does*.' There was an irritable movement at the other side of the room. 'Goodnight.'

Jack straightened his bedclothes out, trying not to be noisy. His dreams had never been like this before. This was something new. Something new and altogether unpleasant.

'Tom?'

'I'm asleep.'

Jack lay back on his pillow, staring up at the wells of darkness that patterned the ceiling. It was a long time before he dared close his eyes again.

'Oh, rats!' hissed Frankie. 'I'm never going to get this right.' She flexed her fingers and tried the complicated run down the guitar fretboard yet again. A cascade of notes chimed loudly from her amplifier.

'Hah! Yessss!' Frankie grinned. Perfect!

It was Saturday morning and Frankie was enjoying the rare luxury of practising on her electric guitar while the house was empty. Dad and Samantha had taken Tabitha with them to the supermarket. If Frankie wanted to play her guitar when they were in the house, she had to use headphones, and playing a blistering heavy-metal lead-guitar solo under a pair of headphones just didn't sound right.

Samantha was Frankie's stepmother. Her own mother had died when she was two years old. Her father had been dating Samantha for the past couple of years, and last year they had got married – two months before Tabitha was born.

Frankie found it very difficult to cope with a woman who suddenly moved in on her and her father, and who seemed to think she was in a position to give Frankie orders. And now the house was full of baby-smells and baby-noise and baby-mess and Frankie almost felt like an outsider in her own home.

Frankie picked up the remote and pointed it at her sound system. A wall of heavy metal music blasted out. Her favourite group: Gorgonhead. Her favourite track: Pegasus War Dance. She waited for the guitar solo to start, then played along, doubling the volume of noise and giving whoops of joy when she got the tricky bits right.

Her best friend, Katie, said this was music for morons. So what? Katie preferred girlie-pop and pretty boy groups. Huh! *Pathetic*!

Frankie let the last high-pitched electronic shriek hang in the air while she picked up the remote and got ready to play the whole thing again.

In the brief quiet, she heard the door bell chime.

She looked at her watch. 'Oops!' It was gone half

past ten, and she'd promised Jack and Tom that she'd be ready if they called on her at that time.

The three of them had arranged to meet up with Regan at the bus station in the town centre. They were planning a second trip to Bodin Summerley and to the dig at The Wicker Man. It would be great research material for their project.

Frankie flew around her room, switching everything off and then bounding down the stairs three at a stretch.

'About time!' declared Tom 'We've been ringing for hours.'

'Sorry. I didn't hear.'

'I'm not surprised,' said Jack. 'What were you doing – strangling cats up there? We could hear the racket from the other end of the street.'

Frankie slammed the door. 'I shall treat that remark with the contempt it deserves,' she said as they walked along the road. 'You just don't know brilliant music when you hear it.'

'Brilliant music?' said Tom. 'You've got to be joking.'

'Now look here . . .'

The argument continued until they got to the bus station. Regan dismissed the whole thing by declaring that hard-core techno-hip-hop was the only real music to listen to.

The bus set off a few minutes later. Yesterday's threatened rain had never materialized and the sky was clear and blue as the bus rumbled its steady way through the woods and farmlands towards Bodin Summerley.

They got off opposite the arcade of shops.

The time-worn old piebald pub sagged and slumbered in the spring sunlight, a little way further along the road.

'Hold on a minute before we go over,' said Frankie, looking around. 'I'm a bit peckish.' She headed towards a little general store that looked like something out of an old-fashioned picture book. The others trailed after her. The shop smelled of lavender and powdered sugar.

A white-haired, elderly lady stood smiling behind the counter. She looked as mild and gentle as a lily. The four friends deposited crisps, chocolate bars and cans of drink in front of her and started searching for money.

'Well, now, so you're the party of young people who helped Mr Fox yesterday when he had his funny turn, hmm?' said the woman in a sweet, soft voice. It made Jack think of cooing doves.

'Hey, that's right,' said Regan in surprise. 'How did you know that?'

The old lady smiled. 'Happy news has winged feet, my dear,' she said. She leaned forwards over the counter. 'Godfrey is an old and very dear friend of mine. And so is Edgar Lovejoy. Our three families have lived in Bodin Summerley for time out of mind.' She nodded brightly. 'I'm Florella Tatum. Miss Florella Tatum. The Foxes and the Lovejoys and the Tatums: we're the three oldest families in the village. Oh, yes, we have very long roots. Roots almost as old and strange as this strange old place itself.' She chuckled. 'And this strange old village has been here for a dreadfully long time, you know.'

'And is it strange?' asked Frankie. She laughed. 'I love the idea of strange old places.'

Miss Tatum leaned even further over the counter. 'Well,' she whispered, 'do you know, they do say, way back in the old days, people hereabouts used to offer blood sacrifices to the elder gods. My own ancestors were druids, if you can believe it. So my granny told me. And the same is true of Godfrey and Edgar, too. We're all of ancient druid stock, by all accounts.' She straightened up with a crystal laugh. 'What do you think of that, eh?'

'Far out,' murmured Regan.

'Our forefathers led the blood sacrifices,' chortled the old lady. 'On May Day. Wonderful May Day! I'm so glad we've revived it. Godfrey, Edgar and I have been asked to organize the whole thing. It's just like the old days. Oh, and of course you'll all be helping with the festival on Monday, hmm?'

Frankie looked at the others. 'We were thinking of coming along to watch,' she said. 'But do you mean we could actually join in?'

'Why, you simply *must*,' said the old lady. 'There will be parades and music and dancing and' – her eyes sparkled – 'feasting!' Her gazed fixed on Frankie. 'And you, my dear, will make the most *beautiful* May Queen.' Frankie went bright red. 'I was the May Queen myself,' continued the old lady. 'Oh, a long, long time ago. Before the festival died out.' She reached out a long, slender hand and held Frankie's wrist. 'You must say yes, my dear. And you must let me show you the ropes. There are lines to be learned and a special costume to be worn.'

'Well, um . . . I suppose I could . . .' Frankie stammered, under the disarming gaze of the old lady. 'But we . . .'

'And you, young man . . .' The old lady's eyes fixed on Jack. 'You must be Jack! You really must!'

'Yes, I am,' Jack said in confusion. What did she mean: *You really must?*

'Jack-in-the-Green!' said the old lady.

'I'm sorry?'

The old lady laughed. 'We need a beautiful young lady and a handsome young man to complete the line-up of characters for the festivities. Your lovely friend here shall be the May Queen, and you shall be Jack-in-the-Green – and at the end of the day, you'll be burned on the Beltane bonfire, just like in the old days!'

Jack stared at her in utter disbelief.

'Wow,' murmured Regan. 'Way to end a party, Jack!'

CHAPTER SIX

First Blood Spilled

'**O**h, come on, Jack,' said Regan. 'You didn't think she meant they'd really dump you on the bonfire at the end?'

'No, of course not.'

The four friends were heading over to The Wicker Man.

'So why the reluctance to be Jack-in-the-Green?' Regan persisted.

'I agreed, didn't I?' Jack said irritably.

'Yeah, *eventually*,' said Regan. 'I don't see what the problem is, Jack. I thought you were really into all this Celtic stuff. And this is real hands-on experience. Tinkerbell will be totally impressed. It'll be mega to the max, guys!'

Before leaving the small village shop, the four friends had agreed to help out all they could with the festival; all they could – Regan said with a cackle of laughter – short of being burned alive as the grand finale!

Miss Tatum seemed to find this remark quite funny. Jack didn't, although he said nothing and finally agreed to take on the role of Jack-in-the-

Green just to keep the others quiet. He wasn't looking forward to it. Jack wasn't a natural performer.

They rounded the back corner of The Wicker Man. Molly and Luke were crouched by the big heap of earth, their heads low as they trailed their fingers through an upended bucket of muddy soil.

'Hi, there!' called Frankie. 'Found anything else?'

Molly looked round. 'Not yet. Nothing new.'

A window opened in the back wall of the pub and Mr Lovejoy's rosy-cheeked face popped out like some kind of exotic fruit.

'Aha!' he crowed. 'Our sacrificial offerings approach! Excellent!'

Frankie stared at him. 'How on earth did you know—' The window slammed before she could finish her question.

Regan peered down the deep hole to see Philip Milligan coming up the ladder with a bucket of earth hooked under one arm.

'Let me,' she said, reaching down to relieve him of the burden. 'How's tricks?'

'Hello, everyone,' he said. 'Nothing as exciting as yesterday, I'm afraid, but it's early days yet.' He clambered out of the gaping hole. 'Take the bucket over to Molly and Luke, please, Regan.'

'Can we help at all?' asked Frankie.

'Certainly you can, if you don't mind getting filthy. You can help Luke and Molly search through the spoil-heap. There may be some shards of pottery or bits of bone I didn't spot.' He jerked a thumb towards the well mouth. 'It's easy to miss stuff down there, even with a lamp.'

Mr Lovejoy came rolling around the side of the building, carrying a large tray. On it were ham and cheese rolls and tumblers and a big jug of lemonade. 'Refreshments for the workers,' he said. He beamed at the four friends.

'Well?' he said. 'Are you up for it, eh? Are you going to help us out?' His eyes sparkled. 'I saw you – from the window – coming out of Miss Tatum's shop. She must have told you what we discussed last night. We all got together at Godfrey's house – Mr Fox's house – last night – all three of us on the festival committee. We had a long talk about you young-sters.' He looked at Frankie. 'I told them – she's a real stunner, the lass with the long golden hair. Pretty as a picture – the perfect May Queen.' His eyes shifted to Jack. 'And the lad, Jack, I told them, well, if he wasn't born to play Jack-in-the-Green, then my name isn't Edgar Percival Archibald Lovejoy!'

Regan coughed and gave Mr Lovejoy a very pointed look.

Mr Lovejoy peered at her for a moment before catching on. 'And those other two,' he said. 'Tom and Ree ... um ... Rurrr ...'

'Regan,' said Regan.

'Yes, yes! Regan, of course.' He smiled like a piano. 'They'll be excellent, too, I don't have the least doubt.' He put the tray down on one of the wooden benches and slapped his big hands together. 'Well?' he said. 'Are you willing?'

'Yes,' said Frankie. 'it sounds great.'

'Excellent,' said Mr Lovejoy. He winked at them. 'It's really not on to pick a sacrifice from your own village, you know. Much better to find willing victims from somewhere else. We don't like to slaughter our own youngsters – it creates such an uproar at the parish council.' He gave a bellow of laughter.

'Yeah, cute joke,' said Regan. 'But can't you come

up with some reason to burn Tom, too? I bet he feels real left out of it.' She grinned. 'I'll supply the matches.'

Before anyone had the chance to follow this up, they were all startled by a long-drawn wail from across the wasteland behind the pub. A middle-aged woman appeared at the back door of Mr Fox's cottage. Even at that distance they could see how distraught she was.

'Oh! Oh! Oh! Help! Help me somebody! It's Mr Fox! He's been attacked! I think he's dying. Oh, please, help!'

'There you go.' Frankie crouched by the big sagging armchair and handed the white-faced old gentleman a steaming mug of tea. 'That should make you feel better.'

'Thank you,' mumbled Mr Fox. 'You're very kind. I'm sorry to be such a nuisance.'

They were in Mr Fox's cottage. The woman who had called for help was his next-door neighbour. She often did a bit of shopping for him and had her own key. She'd let herself in that morning to find the elderly man sprawled on the living room floor, bleeding from a small cut on the back of his head and as still as a stone.

Everyone who had heard her cries had run to help. Frankie had out-sprinted them all and had been the first at Mr Fox's side. A wave of relief had flooded over her when she had heard him groan. At least he wasn't dead.

Remembering her first aid, she had checked there were no broken bones or other injuries before helping the whey-faced old man to sit up.

By then the others had arrived, cramming anxiously into the little living room.

Mr Fox had been unable to offer any detailed explanation for what had happened. He had entered the room and had been struck down from behind by an unseen assailant.

A wave of shock had swept through the people gathered in the little cottage. Mr Lovejoy had picked up the phone to call the police and the neighbour had been sent to the kitchen to make a pot of tea.

'My dear, poor, fellow,' said Mr Lovejoy as Mr Fox sipped the hot tea. 'I can't believe that a thing like this could happen. Not here. Not in Bodin Summerley. A man attacked in his own home – it's . . . it's . . . unthinkable! It'll be some vicious thief from out of the village, you mark my words.'

Mr Fox's voice was shaky. 'I must have disturbed him before he had the chance to steal anything,' he said. He patted the breast of his jacket. 'My wallet is still there.' He cast his rheumy eyes around the room. 'And nothing seems to have been taken.'

'Well, that's lucky, at least,' said Philip Milligan. 'If you can call being hit over the head *lucky*. Would you like us to have a quick scout around – just to check he didn't get into any of your other rooms?'

'Would you, please?' mumbled Mr Fox. 'I'd be most grateful. I hate to be a nuisance.'

'Nonsense!' said Philip Milligan. 'It won't take a jiffy. Come on, Luke – Molly. Let's have a check around.'

'You might like to take a glance into the cellar,' Mr Fox called weakly. 'Just to make sure your relic is safe. Here's the key.'

Regan came back into the room from a quick tour of downstairs doors and windows.

'There's no obvious place where the guy could have gotten in,' she announced. 'The windows are all shut and the front and back door-locks are intact. I checked.'

'I bet you stuck your fingers all over everything,' said Tom. 'The police forensic people will just love you when they arrive – ruining all the evidence: fingerprints and stuff.'

'I didn't touch anything, for your information,' said Regan. 'I'm not totally *dumb*.'

'How long ago did the attack happen?' Jack asked Mr Fox. 'Just a few minutes? I mean, might the burglar still be nearby?'

Mr Fox looked at the watch on this thin wrist. 'It was at least two hours ago,' he said. 'I came in here to fetch my reading glasses.' He pointed towards the mantelpiece. 'And I was struck from behind.' He shook his head. 'I didn't see the person at all.'

'Two hours,' muttered Mr Lovejoy, frowning thunderously. 'My poor chap – two hours!' He strode to the window and stared out. 'The police should be here in a moment. They'll get to the bottom of this.'

Philip Milligan appeared at the door. 'Mr Fox? Exactly *where* in the cellar did you put the head?'

Mr Fox stared confusedly at him. 'It's in full sight – at the foot of the stairs – on the old white cabinet. Isn't it there?'

Philip Milligan's face darkened. 'No,' he said grimly. 'It isn't. And the lock on the cellar door has been forced.'

'Well, I'll be damned!' burst out Mr Lovejoy.

Philip Milligan walked slowly into the room. 'Well,' he breathed angrily. 'I think that solves the question of what the attacker was after. He wanted that head, and he didn't seem to care very much what he had to do to get it!'

'I had no idea archaeology was so cut-throat,' said Frankie. 'I mean: people breaking into people's houses and knocking them unconscious, for heaven's sake!'

'Well, you heard what Philip said,' added Jack. 'There are unscrupulous collectors around who'd pay a lot of money for something as old and as rare as that horse's head.'

'I hope it hauls off and bites him,' said Regan. 'That's what I hope!'

Tom sighed. 'I wish that policeman had let us stay in the cottage – I've never seen a forensic team at work. It would have been dead interesting.'

The four friends were sitting on the low wall that marked the boundary between the pub garden and the wasteland that backed onto Mr Fox's cottage.

Half an hour had gone by since the police had arrived. After passing on the basic facts, the anxious landlord had taken Mr Fox off to the nearest hospital to have his injury properly checked. Philip Milligan had gone with the police officers back to the station in Lychford to give a full description of the missing object. (The expression on the police officers' faces had been extraordinary when they had been told exactly what had been stolen. *I'm sorry, sir – a mummified WHAT?*) Luke and Molly had gone off somewhere together.

After being ejected from the cottage, the four friends had been left to their own devices, to snack on the food they had bought at Miss Tatum's shop and to sit around discussing the unpleasant turn of events. And to wonder what would happen next.

'I hope this doesn't make them cancel the festival,' mused Regan. 'It'd be just typical if they did! I was really looking forward to seeing Jack done up in his party gear.'

'Oh, charming,' said Tom. 'Poor old Mr Fox has his head caved in, and all you're worried about is missing out on a party.'

'Get out of here!' scoffed Regan. 'His head wasn't caved in. It was just a scratch. I've done worse than that falling off – hey! What's that? Look, you guys, *look*!'

She rose to her feet, pointing out across the wasteland, to an open area beyond the huddle of cottages. Thick woodland filled the gap, deep with shadows even in the noonday sunlight.

Frankie turned and followed the line of Regan's pointing finger. Something was moving through the trees. Something large and brown, moving on four legs.

'It's a deer!' said Tom.

'No it isn't,' said Frankie. 'It's too heavy to be a deer.'

'A horse?' said Jack, straining his eyes to make sense of the flickering dappled shape. 'Or a pony, maybe?'

Suddenly the animal broke out of the trees. It was a pony – a small, rough-haired pony, no more than 12 or 13 hands high.

'Cool!' breathed Regan. 'Do you think it'd let me feed it from my hand? Do they eat chocolate?'

The pony trotted out from under the shadows of the woods, its head rising and dipping as it moved in a sure line towards them. All four of them were now standing, staring over the wall as the pony came nearer.

A few metres out from the edge of the wood, the animal stopped.

'He's beautiful,' whispered Frankie, afraid that a loud voice might frighten it away. 'But he's so wild-looking – as if he's never been groomed in his life.' She stepped carefully over the wall, one arm out-stretched.

'Here boy, here,' she crooned. 'Don't be afraid. We won't hurt you.'

'It must belong to someone, surely?' said Tom. 'Do you think it got loose, somehow? Maybe we should grab it, Frankie? There might be a reward.'

'Grab it *how*?' said Jack. 'There's no bridle.'

'Maybe it's some kind of mustang,' said Regan. 'You know – a wild horse.'

'Around here?' Frankie said quietly. 'Hardly. Tom's probably right – he's got loose from some-where.' The crooning tone came back into her voice. 'Here, boy. Here. Tchk-tchk-tchk! There's a beautiful boy. Tchk-tchk!'

The pony flared its nostrils and snorted, its fore-hoof striking the ground once, twice, three times. Then it shook its head and its rugged mane flew.

'Frankie,' murmured Jack. 'There's something strange . . .' His voice petered out. For a split second the animal's huge dark eyes seemed to focus on him, and, even at that distance, Jack saw – or thought he saw – a fleck of red fire that moved in the depths of those great fathomless black pupils.

Then the pony gave a second snort and turned away, presenting its sturdy, rough-haired hind-quarters to them. The ragged tail flicked. The head swung as if beckoning them on, and the pony trotted very deliberately back into the woods.

As though in a dream, and without any clear idea

of why they should do it, the four friends found themselves following the animal into the shadows that lurked under the dense green canopy of interlocking branches.

CHAPTER SEVEN

Into the Haunted Wood

'Hey!' shouted Tom. 'Hey, Jack! *Jack*! Where are you?'

He stared around himself in total confusion. He was in a world of trees. He turned. He couldn't even see where the woods started. And yet . . . and yet he was sure that he had only taken two or three steps into the wood.

'What's going on here!' he shouted. 'Hey! Where is everybody?'

Only ten seconds ago – he was certain it could be no longer than that – he had stepped in under the trees with Jack and Frankie on one side, and Regan on the other. So where on earth were they?

'Ja-ack! Fra-a-a-ankie-e-e-e! Re-e-e-e-ega-a-a-an!'

The endless ranks of silent trees blotted up his voice.

He fought down a crawling panic. This was impossible! His brother and his friends couldn't have just vanished into thin air. He breathed steadily, slowly, horribly aware of the blood pounding through his body.

He turned in a slow circle, peering intently

through the measureless ranks of trees, watching for any break in the monotony of trunks and leaf-laden branches, for any glimpse of movement. For a way out!

The only obvious result of this panoramic survey of the woodland, was that he now had even less idea which way was forwards and which way back.

'Ja-a-a-a-a-a-ck!' His voice cracked with the effort. It hurt his throat. He listened for some distant reply, for some hint of a direction in which to run. But the silence came rolling in over him like an ocean wave.

Tom stiffened. Was that something? He fancied he had heard a sound of movement. The thud of a hoof? The rustle of something brushing elusively through undergrowth.

Once again, he stared all around himself.

The woods were as still as if every tree were a gravestone.

A burst of noise tore through the watching silence. Tom spun on his heel. The pony had come out of nowhere. It was charging straight at him, head down, eyes blazing. Tom lurched to one side and the galloping pony struck him a glancing blow, throwing him to the ground.

Tom tucked himself into a ball, his knees in his chest, his arms up to protect his head. It was a few moments before he even realized that the wood had become silent again.

He lifted a cautious eye over the barrier of his arm.

The pony had vanished.

He stood up, shivering. His ribs ached from the impact of the pony in his side.

He began to run, stumbling over ridges and roots

and tussocks of dead grass, his hand pressed against his bruised ribs, his breath panting, his eyes staring wildly.

Only one thought filled his head: he had to get out of there!

Regan stopped dead in her tracks, eyes narrowing suspiciously.

'Hey, what's the deal here?' she murmured to herself. Had she fallen asleep standing up, or what? Where the heck had Tom gone? One second he'd been right there at her side, and the next – *zippo!* – gone!

She yanked a hunk of her jet black hair off her face and looked over her shoulder. The trees marched off every which way.

'Maybe I had some kind of blackout?' she said aloud. 'Whoo! Cool! My brain's playing tricks on me. Wait till I tell the guys.' She took another look over her shoulder. She had the feeling that someone, or *something*, was watching her.

'That kind of thing could turn out real handy,' she said, as though speaking to some invisible friend – as though she was having a perfectly ordinary conversation in a perfectly ordinary place. 'If I could blank stuff out on purpose, I'd be able to miss all the boring classes at school. That would be so neat!'

All the time that she was speaking, her eyes were darting through the endless files of tree trunks for some way out of the woods.

The feeling of being watched was like a hand pressing between her shoulder blades; like hot animal breath on her neck. But whatever was watching her, she didn't want it to know she was scared.

Maybe if it thought she couldn't care less, it would go away – and then she could figure a route out of this place!

'Gee,' she said loudly, her voice quivering a little. 'This sure is *fun*!' She swallowed past a thick lump in her throat. 'I wouldn't have missed this for the world!'

She suddenly felt that the watching *thing* wasn't fooled at all.

'Hey! Tom, Jack, Frankie! I hope you're having as good a time as I am!' she shouted. The branches seemed to snatch her words out of the air, killing them and throwing them ineffectually at her feet.

'Oh, heck!' she sighed. 'Something totally weird is going on here.' She took a deep breath. 'OK, whoever you are, I'm real impressed!' she yelled. 'You've gotten my attention, OK? Do you wanna come out and *do* whatever it is you do?'

The woodland held its breath.

'Hey, sad-guy, show yourself, huh?' Regan shouted. 'I'm getting *bo-ored*! Helloo-oo? Regan to scary-person: this is, like, really *boring*!'

An explosion of noise erupted behind her. She turned. The wild pony was rearing up right on top of her, its hooves like iron mallets pounding down to break her bones, its lips drawn back to reveal an evil yellow grin, its blazing eyes filled with malice.

Regan threw her arms up and let out a scream of pure terror, certain that within a split second one of those raging hooves would come down and kick her brains clear through the back of her head.

Silence. Silence, except for the roller-coaster rhythm of blood beating in her temples. She opened an eye.

The pony was gone. Wild eyes, grinning teeth,

hammering hooves: all gone as if they had never been there.

Regan scraped a curtain of hair off her face. 'Well,' she breathed, 'I guess I asked for that.'

Her legs felt very strange. Leaves danced darkly against the sky.

The next thing she knew, she was sitting in the mess and litter of the woodland floor with the trees swimming around her head.

She gave herself a minute or two to recover, then she clambered to her feet. She fixed her mouth in a determined, silent line and, choosing a direction at random, she set off into the trees.

Jack held back from entering the wood. He wasn't certain whether or not he had imagined that lick of fire in the pony's eyes, but it had made him uneasy all the same.

He was one pace back from Frankie. Tom and Regan were over to his right. He saw the pony move in under the trees and saw it dissolve away into nothing, like breath on glass.

The melting away of the animal was so utterly astonishing that it took Jack a couple of seconds to get his head around what he had seen. Had it been a trick of the strange green light under the branches? Shadows playing games with his eyes? Camouflage? No! It had been none of those things. The animal had simply bled out of existence in the time it took to draw a breath.

Tom and Regan stepped into the woods.

'No!' Jack lunged forwards, catching hold of Frankie's arm. She tugged against his grip, neither turning her head nor crying out as she struggled to get in under the trees.

'Tom! Don't!' But it was too late. Tom and Regan were gone.

Frankie's fingers worked to prise Jack's hand off her arm.

He pulled at her with all his strength – she was dragging him in under the awning of rustling, whispering branches. And she was so *strong*!

'Frankie! Stop it! Don't go in there!' She was already in the shadow of the wood. If he didn't release her, she'd just tow him in after her. '*Frankie*!'

At last she turned to stare at him. Her expression was blank, her eyes glassy and drained of colour – clear, like water. Whatever was looking at him through her eyes, it wasn't Frankie.

'Let ... me ... go ...' The voice was slow and deep and resonant and, although Frankie's mouth moved, the actual sound seemed to come booming up out of the ground.

The shock of it almost made Jack lose his grip. But he pulled himself together and prepared for one last effort. He wrapped his free arm around a tree trunk and dug his heels in. Her fingernails raked down the back of his hand, but he was ready. He released her for a second and, as she surged forwards, he hooked his fingers into the waistband of her jeans in the small of her back and gave one last, great heave.

For a moment he was afraid that he'd lost her: she was reaching forwards and her arms had evaporated up to the elbows.

But suddenly the strength seemed to drain out of her and he was able to drag her clear of the trees. They tumbled into the grass together in a tangle of arms and legs. Jack wrapped his arms tightly around her and clung on with all his might.

'Jack!' Frankie's voice was shrill in his ear. 'What are you *doing?*'

She squirmed in his arms.

'Jack! You're squishing me!' It was her own voice again. Jack relaxed his arms a little and looked into her face. Her eyes were sea-grey and full of intelligence.

With a gasp of relief, he let her go. She sat up, straightening her clothes. She looked down at him, sprawling breathlessly in the long grass.

'What on earth are you playing at?' she demanded. 'You could've done me a mischief! Are you out of your tiny mind?'

Jack jumped up. 'We've got to get Tom and Regan back!' he gasped. 'They've gone in there. I couldn't stop them.'

'Jack – what are you talking about?'

He stared at her. 'Don't you remember?'

'Remember? Remember what?' She scrambled to her feet. 'Oh, yes! The *pony.* We were following the pony.' She frowned. 'And then you grabbed me from behind.'

Jack ran to the outer margins of the wood.

'Tom! Regan!' he shouted into the shadows, running this way and that along the unfriendly front ranks of trees.

Baffled, Frankie ran after him. 'Jack! Will you please tell me what's going on!'

'The pony just vanished,' he said distractedly. 'Then Tom and Regan vanished. And you nearly vanished, too, but I had hold of you. Except . . . except that it wasn't *you.*' He stared at her with eyes brimming with horror. 'Frankie. I don't know what to do. I don't know how to get them back. I think . . . I think they might be gone for ever!'

CHAPTER EIGHT
Ancient Rites

'This isn't happening. This isn't happening.' As he ran, Tom kept muttering that urgent wish to himself over and over again, as if the repetition might make it true. '*This isn't happening!*'

The trees crowded all around him like people in a nightmare who shutter their faces and turn their backs when you cry for help.

Tom gasped in shock and came crashing down onto his knees. The trees had gone. One second his eyes had been full of woodland – the next he was stumbling through open grass with the familiar shape of The Wicker Man only fifty or so metres away.

'Oh! Thank heavens!' He knelt on all fours in the long friendly grass, sucking in air and panting out relieved laughter.

'Tom!'

He lifted his head. Jack and Frankie were running towards him – they looked as freaked-out as he felt!

Tom stood up. He swayed a little.

'What happened?' gasped Jack as they reached him. 'Are you OK?'

'I'm fine. I got lost... and...' He gave his brother a puzzled look. Suddenly he realized why Jack didn't like to talk about his weird dreams. 'I don't know what happened,' he said. 'I got confused. Where's Regan?'

'She's still *in* there,' said Jack. 'How did you get out?'

'I ran.'

'Did you meet anything in there?' Jack asked.

'The pony was there,' said Tom. He rubbed his ribs. 'It knocked me over. I think it's *mental* or something.'

'He's probably frightened to death,' said Frankie. 'We ought to try and find him.'

'I really wouldn't go in there,' said Tom, staring at the bland face of the woodland.

Frankie looked at him. 'Why not?'

A high-pitched shriek came slicing through the air. 'Eeyahhhwhoooo!' All heads turned. About a hundred metres away, they saw Regan at the edge of the wood, yelling at the top of her voice, jumping up and down and punching the air.

'In your *face*, freaky *place*!' she hollered.

She waved and came running towards them, skipping into the air every few steps and continuing her raucous victory chant.

'You're not gonna *believe* what's just happened to me!' she yelled. 'That place is, like, totally haunted! It was *awesome!*'

Regan gave them a breathless account of the strange way the woods seemed to spread out for ever in all directions, and of her clash with the mysterious pony.

'And then I thought, I'm out of here, man!' she said, 'And, like, a couple of minutes later I was back in the real world again. Listen, if you want my opinion, that horse is some kind of a *ghost* horse.' Her voice lowered to a sepulchral whisper. 'And that wood is a *portal to another dimension.*'

Frankie gaped at her. 'The pony was *real*,' she said. 'I saw him.'

'And I saw him disappear,' Jack said quietly. 'I don't know about other dimensions, but something weird is going on.'

'Maybe we should tell someone,' said Regan.

'They'll think we're crackers,' said Tom.

'Not if other people have had weird encounters in there,' said Regan. She stared in through the trees. 'Maybe one of us should go back in and check it out, huh?'

'Not me!' said Tom.

'Me neither,' agreed Jack. 'But I think Regan's right – we ought to try and find out if there are any local legends about this place.'

'I'd like to point out right here and now,' Frankie said very determinedly, 'that I don't believe in ghosts. And I *definitely* don't believe in other dimensions!'

'Fine,' said Tom. 'In you go, then. It's been nice knowing you.'

'I will, too!' Frankie said determinedly.

'No, don't!' said Jack.

Regan shook her head. 'I really wouldn't,' she said. 'That horse nearly took my head off. Jack's right – we need to find out if anyone else has had weirdo experiences around here.'

'I'd rather not know,' Tom said quietly. 'I'd rather forget the whole thing.'

Regan faced him with her hands on her hips. 'Well, of all the *wussy* attitudes . . .'

'Maybe Tom's right,' said Jack. 'Listen, I think we

need to get away from here for a while. If only to clear our heads a bit.' He turned to Regan. 'This isn't just fun, you know. When I tried to stop Frankie going into the wood, something *looked* at me from right inside her. I don't know what it was, but it was very old and it was . . .' his voice faded to a breath, '. . . it was very *dangerous*.'

Regan opened her mouth but closed it again without speaking. She looked enquiringly at Frankie.

Frankie shook her head. 'I don't know what to think,' she said.

'While we're deciding, can we get further away from *that*?' Tom said, glancing apprehensively at the rustling woodland. The olive shadows seemed seeded with eyes.

'Yes,' said Jack. 'And I know what we can do. Let's get the next bus back to town and take a look in the library. Frankie? Have you got Darryl's book list for the project?'

'Right here,' said Frankie, patting the seat of her jeans. 'I agree with Jack – let's go and do some research.'

'I hope we find something about local haunted woods,' said Regan as they headed for the bus stop. 'And local phantom horses.'

'I hope we don't,' Tom mumbled to himself.

The library in Lychford was housed in a big rambling old red-brick building that had once been a school. Mrs Christmas wasn't on duty, but the assistant librarian directed the friends to the room where academic books were kept.

They managed to find seven books from Darryl's list, some big and user-friendly and filled with illustrations, some stumpy and thick and full of intimidatingly dense writing. They spread them out on the long mahogany table and began to work their way through them. Frankie tore pages out of her notebook so they could scribble down useful bits of information as they went along.

'I've found something,' said Tom after a few minutes. 'Some May Day festivals include a thing called a Horn Dance, where people dress up in animal skins and wear the antlers and horns of animals, and dance through the streets. It's supposed to help with hunting.'

'Whoa! Hold the presses!' Regan said with a laugh. 'This is brilliant. Apparently there's a tradition called *Beating the Bounds*. Nowadays it involves people walking around a village or town and whacking special stones or trees with sticks. But in the old days' – she grinned at Tom – 'they used to take the village boys out and whack them instead. It sounds like a totally sensible custom – I think we should revive it. How about it, Tom? You and me, huh?'

'I don't think so,' said Tom. 'But I've just seen the perfect role for you to play. The Fool. You have to dress up in a silly costume and prance around the village with a balloon on the end of a stick, acting like a total idiot.' He returned her fake grin. 'Think you could manage that?'

'I dunno,' said Regan. 'Maybe if you gave me a few tips on what it's like to *be* a total idiot?'

'Oh, give over, you two,' said Jack. 'You're not fooling anyone. Everyone knows you like each other really.'

'Wha-at!' howled Regan and Tom in mutual outrage.

'I've found something about the May Queen,' said Frankie. 'She wears a costume of red and white and

64

is garlanded with flowers. Then she leads the parade through the village streets and sits at the foot of the maypole while the dancing goes on.'

'Do they have a maypole in Bodin Summerley?' wondered Jack.

'Perhaps they'll put one up specially,' said Tom.

'Or maybe they do different stuff,' suggested Regan. 'According to this book here, there's heaps of different ways of celebrating Beltane. In some villages they roll a burning wheel down a hill. In another they have to turn a huge stone over.'

'Why?' asked Tom.

'Beats me,' said Regan. 'In one village they even roll a big cheese down a hill and the village boys have to try and catch it.' She looked from Tom to Jack to Frankie. 'You Brits sure are strange.'

'The one thing they all seem to have in common,' said Frankie, 'is the fact that they all light bonfires. In some places they have whole rows of bonfires on all the surrounding hilltops. That must look amazing when the sun goes down.' She glanced up. 'Jack? Are you OK? You look ill.'

As Frankie had spoken of the hill-top string of bonfires, the terrible dream had flooded into Jack's mind like a black tide.

'Yes, fine,' he said. He took a deep breath and tried to smile. 'Headache,' he explained. 'All this small print. I think I'll take a walk. It'll clear my head a bit.'

Tom looked at him in concern.

'I'll tell you what you can do, if you're sick of reading,' said Regan. 'You could go back to Bodin Summerley and find out what's the deal with the festival. We left without speaking to anyone. We need to know exactly what they want us to do and when they want us to do it.'

'And you can ask after Mr Fox,' said Frankie. 'And have a word with Philip Milligan. And you could . . .' She paused, as though carefully weighing her words. 'You could . . . check stuff out . . . you know?'

Jack knew what she meant. *Excuse me, are there any haunted woods or phantom ponies around these parts? Why do I ask? Oh, no reason – I just wondered . . .*

Jack didn't much like the idea of a return visit to Bodin Summerley. But then a favourite expression of his mother's glided through his head. *The fear that is never confronted can never be defeated.*

He got up. 'OK,' he said. 'I suppose we do need to find out what's happening over there. Coming, Tom?'

Tom kept his head down. 'Um . . . no . . . actually. I think I'll carry on with this.'

'Fine. See you later, then.' He gave the two girls a brief smile. 'I'll give you a ring to let you know what's going on.'

With that, Jack was gone.

Tom felt guilty about leaving his brother to go back alone, but he couldn't face it right then. He'd go with Jack tomorrow. Tomorrow would be fine. The memory would have faded a bit by then. He glanced up, half-expecting reproachful looks from the girls. But they were busy reading.

'Here we go,' said Regan. 'Jack-in-the-Green.' She flattened out a page with the heel of her hand and began to read. '*Jack-in-the-Green is a central figure in many Beltane festivities. The chosen person would be completely encased in a bell-shaped wickerwork frame entwined with branches, leaves and flowers. He would be guided around the village accompanied by music and singing,*

66

and at the end of the ceremonies he would be carried to the bonfire and symbolically burned.' She looked across the table at Tom. 'You'd better tell your brother to put on his best asbestos underwear, man. It's gonna be some party!'

CHAPTER NINE
Phantom Pony
Running Wild

Tom was up in their shared bedroom, deeply into a very complicated computer game when Jack got back from Bodin Summerley later that afternoon. Tom was staring at a chessboard on the screen. He had to arrange eight Queens so there was no crossover either up and down or diagonally. Tricky.

He swivelled in his chair as Jack came in.

'Well, how'd it go?' Tom was feeling much brighter. The sinister forest was losing its grip on him and he was already beginning to think the whole thing had been a trick of the light or some sort of hallucination brought about by eating too many cheese and onion crisps.

Jack threw himself onto his bed. His head was full of distant thunder.

'Mr Milligan had packed up and gone when I got there,' Jack said, his arms across his face. The darkness was soothing. 'They won't be back until Tuesday, apparently. So Mr Lovejoy said.'

'Any news about the horse's head?'

Jack shrugged. 'Mr Lovejoy didn't know anything.

Mr Fox is OK, though. They checked him over in the hospital and they've already let him out.'

'So . . .' Tom said guardedly, ' . . . everything's . . . OK . . . over there . . . huh? Nothing . . . um, nothing's *happened*?'

'No, nothing's happened. And, yes, since you're obviously dying to know, I *did* ask Mr Lovejoy about local legends and stuff.' Jack smiled. 'I got an ear-bashing for about an hour before I could get away. If you believe *him*, then this has got to be the most haunted county in the entire world. Ghost monks, ghost nuns, ghost dogs, ghost cats. Ghosts without heads. Ghosts with two heads. A ghost lady who plays the harp on Easter Sunday, and a ghost bellringer who rings the ghost bells of the ghost church whenever danger threatens the land.'

Tom laughed. 'What about a ghost landlord in the pub?'

'Oh, yeah, I forgot to mention him.' Jack shook his head. 'The only things he didn't mention were a ghost wood and a ghost pony.'

Tom's face became serious. 'So, what do you think it was? What *happened* back there?'

'I haven't got a clue,' said Jack. 'Your guess is as good as mine.'

'Mass hallucination,' said Tom.

Jack smiled. 'Yeah – why not?'

The two brothers looked at one another for a few silent moments, both desperate to believe that nothing really *bad* had happened that afternoon.

Jack was dreading the approaching night. The dreams lurked just beyond the horizons of his mind, only waiting for the darkness to come swarming back.

'So, what's the plan for the festival?' asked Tom.

'I said we'd be there about midday tomorrow,' said Jack. 'That should give us plenty of time to find out what they want us to do on Monday.'

'You're still up for it, then?'

A half-smile slid across Jack's face. 'Do I have any choice? Can you imagine what Frankie and Regan would have to say about it if I backed out now?' He stood up and stretched. 'Anyway, it'll be fine. There'll be tons of people around. Nothing weird's going to happen in the middle of a load of people.' He pushed his dark thoughts away. 'I'm off for a shower.'

Tom turned back to his computer puzzle. Jack was right – what could possibly happen in the middle of a big crowd of celebrating people?

It was Sunday the 30th of April: the Eve of Beltane.

Jack had phoned earlier that morning, to let Regan know the plans for the afternoon. They were all to meet up at the bus station at twelve o'clock. Regan leaned her elbows on the windowsill and stared out over the massive lawns and flowerbeds and sculpted hedges of her new home.

The Vanderlindens were renting a huge, empty, echoing house in the most upmarket part of Lychford. Regan could never figure out why her parents thought they needed so much space – they were never *there*!

Through the open door of her bedroom, she could hear the screechy nasal voice of Jennie St Claire blathering endlessly into the telephone. Jennie was the new au pair – brought over from America to look after Regan – as if Regan needed looking after!

Jennie had three interests: eating, watching talkshows on TV, and making very lengthy international calls to her boyfriend in Los Angeles.

Regan was left more or less to her own devices by Jennie – which suited Regan just fine.

The whiny voice scraped at the inside of Regan's skull.

She stood up. 'That's it! I'm gone. I'm history!' She grabbed a jacket and headed out. She marched past Jennie with only a contemptuous twitch of her eyebrow.

' . . . so, anyway, she was, like, bag your *nails*, they're grody to the max, and I was like, *excuse* me, and she was like – *hey*! Wait a moment, Brad. Regan! Where are you going?'

'Out!'

'Uh-huh? Out where?'

'The North Pole!'

'Oh, right! Super-funny, Regan! Now just you—'

Regan slammed the front door. She'd left the house with no particular idea of what to do – other than to get as far away from that voice as possible – but once she was out in the open an idea hit her.

Why wait till midday? I'll go over to Bodin Summerley right now – maybe I'll catch up with some more spooks before the others scare 'em off!

She looked up into the bright spring sky.

'To heck with the bus,' she said. 'I'll bike over.' It was ages since she'd been on a long bike ride and the thought of the refreshing country wind in her face really appealed to her.

Forty minutes later she was almost there; free-wheeling down a long straight slope of road, her hair flying out behind like a black banner, her lightning-blue eyes screwed against the rush of air, and her over-large mouth stretched in a grin that threatened to meet around the back of her neck. This was great! It was *brilliant*!

She had the whole grey length of the road to herself. It was like there wasn't another living thing for ten kilometres in any direction.

And then she saw it.

She slammed on the brakes and came to a skidding halt.

The road was bordered with hedges, but in a narrow crack between two gouts of fresh spring green, she had seen a small rough-haired brown pony cantering alongside her in a field – as though it was secretly keeping up with her behind the barrier of the hedge.

She threw her bike down at the edge of the road and ran back to the gap in the hedge. She stared through into a field, hemmed with dark green trees and bushes.

There was no sign of the pony.

'Heyyy, what's the big deal?' Her eyebrows knitted. There was nowhere for the pony to have gone.

Imagination. Pure and simple. She chuckled at her own gullibility as she walked back to retrieve her bike. It had flattened some roadside flowers, scattering small white petals.

As she picked her bike up, her eyes were held by something very strange on the ground where it had fallen. On a patch of bare earth, some petals had dropped in such a way as to form the outline of a horse. A running horse.

Regan leaned over her bike, mesmerized by the uncanny picture. The sun burned like animal breath on her neck. The air became deadly still.

A car swept by with a startling roar. The petal-shape stirred in the slipstream of the car and the pattern was blown apart as if it had never been.

Regan shook herself like a wet dog.

Without allowing herself to pause for even a moment of thought, she climbed onto her bike and steadfastly continued the journey to Bodin Summerley. She filled her head with the simple lyric of a favourite song. Over and over. Over and over and over.

In a tiny corner of her mind she knew that if she let herself start thinking about what had just happened, she'd probably turn her bike around right there and then and not stop pedalling until she was back in her bedroom, and safe under her bed!

She came sailing into the village, deeply grateful for the scattering of people and cars and friendly shops; for the picturesque *normality* of it all. Some people were gathered around a tall stepladder, putting up red and yellow bunting, and many windows were already hung with red and yellow banners and streamers.

Regan swooped into the car park of The Wicker Man. The gnarled black doors were still closed but she could see dim rosy lights through the mullioned windows. The pub sign creaked in the breeze.

Regan stared around, her eyes narrowing. There *was* no breeze. The air was warm and still. Not a branch nor a leaf was moving. The painted wicker giant stared down at her, its body filled with struggling people. Mouths open in silent panic, arms stretching out desperately for help.

As if to prove things like that didn't faze her at all, she propped her bike against the pole which supported the sign and strolled nonchalantly around to the back of the pub to see how things were looking at the dig.

She gave the distant woodland a brief glance. It hung against the ground like thick green smoke. Regan swallowed hard and looked away.

The pit was covered by the tarpaulin and surrounded by red and white barrier tape. The tarpaulin sagged into the gaping throat, pinned at the corners by wooden pegs driven into the ground. Jack had told her that Philip Milligan wouldn't be there. Still, that didn't mean a person couldn't take a peek.

To one side lay the spoil-heap mound. The ladder rested on the ground alongside the pub wall.

Regan crouched down and lifted the edge of the tarpaulin. It was heavy. She looked around, feeling a little guilty although she couldn't figure why. It wasn't like anyone had told them that the excavation was a forbidden zone.

She hauled the big tarp up over her shoulders and crawled in underneath. In the cavern made from the humped material, the air was heavy and translucently green, like old air trapped for years in a thick green bottle. Stale air, breathed out by monsters, dank and dreadful.

She glimpsed something that glittered and shone near the curved lip of the well. Glass? Shining shards of flint, maybe, dyed green by the clotted light. She crawled nearer. Flecks and splinters of some green stone were embedded into the raw earth right at the very lip of the gaping black hole.

Regan gasped. The fetid air filled her lungs and made her cough.

The stones formed the shape of a running green horse.

Regan saw a movement between her hands. Something dark and shapeless, like a demonic blob of living slime, suddenly jumped at her face. There was a slithery impact against her cheek. She let out a yelp and lifted her hand to her face.

Her other hand slipped on the damp earth. She had a horrifying moment in which to stare down into that yawning hole before she lost balance and fell into the swallowing darkness.

CHAPTER TEN
Regan and the Toad

'Jack – you look *terrible*!' Frankie's eyes were full of concern as she came marching up to the bus stop where her friend was already waiting.

'Thanks,' said Jack. 'That's just what I needed to hear.'

'Oh. Sorry. But . . .' She scrutinized his face. 'You look like you haven't slept for a week.'

Tom appeared from around a corner where he'd been examining a local route map to pass the time. Jack had been silent and preoccupied all morning, and Tom was beginning to find his brother's unusual gloominess a bit burdensome.

'Bus in five minutes,' said Tom. He looked at Frankie. 'Hi. Do you want to have a go at cheering misery-guts up? He's been a total pain all day. And if you say anything to him he just bites your head off.'

'Hang on a second and I'll do some happy cartwheels for you,' Jack said flatly.

'See what I mean?' Tom said to Frankie.

'Didn't you sleep very well?' asked Frankie.

'No.' Jack didn't mention that he'd deliberately

kept himself awake through much of the night. It had been the only way to keep the dreams at bay. What brief and fitful moments of sleep he had succumbed to, had been full of oppressive black danger and clawing red fire.

'When I can't sleep,' began Frankie. 'I have this routine I go through. I start at the far end of my body, yeah? I say: Foot? Are you listening to me, foot? Foot, you are feeling sleepy. You are feeling *very* sleepy.' She grinned hopefully. 'And then I work my way up.'

'Does that work?' asked Tom.

'Nope,' laughed Frankie. 'But it passes the time.'

Jack smiled.

'It's her own fault if she can't get to places on time,' said Tom as the three of them got off the bus at Bodin Summerley. He was talking about Regan. They hadn't waited for her – the next bus wouldn't have come for an hour. She'd just have to catch up with them later on.

'So you keep saying,' said Frankie. She looked around. 'Wow! Someone's been busy!'

The main street of the village had been transformed. Red and yellow decorations hung from virtually every building, and red and yellow lights stretched to and fro right across the high street on wires, twined about with triangular red and yellow bunting.

Even the grim pub sign had its share of colourful decorations, and the post itself was wound round and round with red and yellow tape, so that it looked like a giant stick of rock.

Someone was experimenting with a loud PA system. Distorted music filled the air.

'Mr Lovejoy said to meet up with them in the church hall,' said Jack. 'It's this way.' He led them away from the pub and towards a lane that darted behind the row of high-street shops.

He suddenly stopped. It had been a curious sensation. A feeling in his head as of something briefly making itself known, before sinking once more under his consciousness.

He stared back across the road.

'What's up?' asked Tom.

'I don't know,' said Jack. He took a couple of halting steps back the way they had come. 'Something . . .'

'Do you feel ill again?' asked Frankie. 'Shall I get you a drink? Do you want to sit down?'

'No, no. It's nothing like that.' Jack felt drawn across the road. He waited for a gap in the steady drizzle of traffic. Tom and Frankie looked at one another. Tom shrugged.

'He gets like this sometimes,' he said.

They trailed after Jack. Suddenly he laughed and pointed. 'She's already here!' he said. He grinned around at them. 'Regan's already here.' He was pointing to Regan's bike. Someone had moved it from the pole and had propped it against the wall.

But as Jack neared the machine, a cold darkness seeped into his mind. Something was wrong. At that moment the blare of music briefly died and Jack heard a distant, muffled yelling.

'Regan!' He ran around to the back of the pub. The music started up again and the voice was drowned.

Jack wrenched the nearest peg out of the ground and dragged the tarpaulin back off the hole.

'About darned *time*!' screeched Regan, her voice

in rags. 'What's a person gotta do to get rescued around here – write the Prime Minister?'

Frankie and Tom came running up. Cautiously Frankie approached the bevelled edge of the shaft. Regan's cross, dirty face stared up out of the depths. She was standing up, ankle-deep in soft earth, smeared and dishevelled and radiating intense annoyance.

'Are you OK?' called Frankie. The shaft had to be at least four metres deep.

'What kind of a dumb question is that?' hollered Regan. 'I've just about yelled my lungs out trying to get help. No one could hear me over that noise! Wait until I get my hands on the dingbat who's responsible for that music!'

Tom looked down the hole. 'How'd you get down there?' he asked.

Regan's fists hit her hips. 'Well, gee, I don't know, Tom. Maybe I *fell*, huh?'

Jack laughed. 'Are you hurt at all?'

'Of course I'm hurt,' bellowed Regan. 'I just fell down a big pit. I hurt all over.'

Jack looked at Frankie. 'She's OK,' he said. 'She wouldn't be making all that noise if she'd done herself any real damage.'

'Hey!' hollered Regan. 'What is this? A hole-staring contest? Is someone gonna get me out of here or what?'

'There's the ladder,' said Tom, pointing. 'I suppose we'd better rescue her.'

The three of them manhandled the long unwieldy ladder to the lip of the well.

'Watch out below!' shouted Frankie as they began to let the ladder down.

'Careful!' came Regan's voice from the depths.

The end of the ladder came wavering down across the ring of blue sky. Regan reached up to fend it off. It swung as her friends tried to control its descent. The foot of the ladder crunched into the wall of the well just above Regan's head and lodged itself.

'Oh, great!' groaned Regan. She jumped up and caught hold of the lowest rung. There was a sudden movement as the ladder freed itself. Regan heard a dull, crumbly, thumping sound. The foot of the ladder had broken through the inner skin of the shaft and had left a ragged black hole, about two metres up from the bottom. A curious smell wafted out. The stale and sweet smell of old beer.

The ladder thudded down.

Regan scrambled onto the ladder and climbed quickly, ignoring the crack in the wall in her hurry to get out of the pit. A few moments later she hit the air.

'Thanks, guys,' she said, staring around at the three questioning faces. 'I thought I was in there for *life*. I gotta tell you – I've been having some really weird experiences this morning.'

The four of them sat on one of the benches behind The Wicker Man while Regan told her story. Cheerful music blasted out across the village – whoever was in charge of the public address system was apparently still not satisfied that it was working properly.

'How I didn't break my neck, I'll never know,' she finished. 'I guess it was because it's all soft and squishy down there.' She plucked at her mud-smeared clothes. The angle of the shaft's walls had helped. The well was shaped like an ice-cream cone, sliced away at one side by the back wall of the pub. It was far too steep and featureless to allow her to save herself, but the wide mouth had given her time to scrabble around and make the worst of the fall into the tapering shaft feet-first. Feet first into ankle-deep ooze.

Jack got up and walked over to the well. He crouched and searched for any sign of the horse of green stones. The deep grooves and scrape marks of Regan's fall were clearly marked. But there was no pattern of stones.

Jack lifted the tarpaulin further back. A fat brown toad blinked stupidly for a moment in unexpected sunlight before crawling back under cover.

Jack smiled. At least one part of Regan's story had a rational explanation. The startled toad must have jumped into her face as she'd crawled in under the tarpaulin. That was her blob of leaping slime. That was how come she'd fallen.

'Yes, fine, I'll buy that,' Regan said when Jack told her about the toad. 'But what about all this *horse* stuff?'

'It's a pony,' said Tom.

'Pony-schmoney!' snapped Regan. 'What we have on our hands, here, guys, is some kind of ghost horse.' She counted on her fingers. 'Yesterday we *all* saw it, and when we followed it into that wood, we were in, like, Freaksville Arizona! It was following me today, *and* I saw a bunch of petals in a horse shape. And right *here* I saw it in green stones. Now, I really don't *care* that the pattern isn't there any more, guys. I *saw* it. And I'm not going crazy!'

'I think Regan's right,' said Jack. 'Whatever else she is, she doesn't strike me as the sort of person to see things that aren't there.'

'Excuse me?' interrupted Regan. 'What exactly do you mean by, *whatever else she is?*'

'You seriously think that the pony we saw yesterday was some sort of ghost?' said Frankie. 'Seriously?'

Jack looked at her. 'Anyone got any better ideas?'

'You mean apart from Regan going loony?' said Tom.

She glared at him. 'Wanna find out what it's like down the bottom of that hole, Tom? Like, head first?'

'He's kidding you,' said Jack. 'We all saw the pony yesterday – it's not just you.' He paused for a moment, gathering his thoughts. 'The thing is,' he said slowly, 'I think I might have an explanation for what's going on here.'

'Good,' said Frankie. 'Let's hear it.'

He eyed her uneasily. 'You won't like it.'

'Try me.'

'I think it's something to do with *that.*' He pointed over to the black gape of the Iron Age shaft. 'I think Philip Milligan has disturbed something that should have been left in peace.'

As he finished speaking, the blaring, tinny music suddenly ceased and an awful silence descended on the village. Tom's voice broke the tension, sounding small and distant.

'I don't think I want to be here any more,' he said. 'I don't think I like this place.'

CHAPTER ELEVEN
Edgar Lovejoy's Herbal Soothing Compound

'Well, well, well, well, well!' The jolly bellow of Mr Lovejoy's voice came crashing into the aching silence. He came barrelling across the garden, grinning like a friendly orang-utan. 'Here we all are, then! And I can get out of doors at last, now Simon's finished assaulting our ears with that infernal racket.' He rubbed his meaty hands together. 'Everyone full of beans and raring to . . . to . . .' He gazed at Regan's grubby clothes. 'My dear young lady, what on *earth* have you been up to?'

'I've taken up all-in mud-wrestling,' Regan intoned hollowly.

'She fell down the pit,' said Tom.

Mr Lovejoy's eyebrows shot up. 'But that's so dangerous!'

'I know,' said Regan.

'You could have been injured.'

'I know,' Regan repeated between gritted teeth.

'You should be much more careful, my dear. If—'

'The thing is,' interrupted Jack, 'we've been having some really strange experiences.' He looked at the others. 'We *all* have.'

'Indeed?' said Mr Lovejoy. 'Do tell – I love stories about strange experiences.'

Backed up by the others, Jack falteringly explained as best he could the events of the past two days. The deeper they got into their narrative, the sillier Frankie felt about the whole thing. Mr Lovejoy must think they were a bunch of hysterical idiots!

Jack stopped short of his theory that the appearances of the pony were linked to the mummified head that had been unearthed from the shaft. That was just *too* weird to try and explain to an adult.

'So?' Frankie looked up into Mr Lovejoy's ruddy face. She smiled embarrassedly. 'We're completely mad, yeah?'

'I still think we should just forget the whole thing and go home,' said Tom. 'This entire place gives me the creeps.'

Mr Lovejoy looked thoughtfully at him. 'What's called for here,' he said slowly, 'is a glass each of Mr Edgar Lovejoy's patent herbal soothing compound. That'll bring the roses back into your cheeks.' He held up a hand. 'Don't move. I'll only be a jiffy. You'll see, the world will look quite different with a drop or two of herbal soothing compound inside you.'

The drink was a creamy pink colour and smelled of peaches.

'Drink it down!' said Mr Lovejoy. 'Every drop!'

'It tastes kind of fuzzy,' said Regan, licking her lips and placing her empty glass back on the tray. 'Sweet and fuzzy . . . like . . . cotton candy . . .' She blinked at the others. For a moment their faces had blurred and swum out of focus.

'What were we talking about?' asked Jack. He felt

as though he'd just woken from a surprise doze under the burning sun.

'We were all about to take a stroll over to the church hall,' said Mr Lovejoy. 'There's plenty to be done. Fun and games!'

'Yeah . . .' Frankie said vaguely. 'Yeah, that was it.'

Tom had the feeling that something important had just dived down beneath his consciousness. Ripples of the forgotten thing spread and faded. It was gone. Whatever it had been, it was gone. They were going to the church hall. Yes, that was it. The church hall.

The entrance to the hall was decked out in yellow and red, and a large hand-painted sign read: *May Day Festival. Craft fair and refreshments. All welcome.*

The long hall was a hive of activity. Stalls were being set up and people were scampering busily about. In one corner a marching band was practising a very ragged version of The Floral Dance. In another space, children in green tunics were being tutored in a simple dance routine.

Mr Lovejoy led the four friends through the throng and up a short flight of steps to the stage that dominated one end of the hall. A group of people were constructing garlands and wreaths of flowers. A fat man was helping a small gang of children to construct a strange, boat-shaped thing, about two metres long, which was in the process of being covered in black material.

Miss Tatum appeared from the wings of the stage. She smiled.

'Oh, excellent!' she said. 'You're here. Now then, Frankie, we need to have a chat about what you'll be expected to do tomorrow.'

'Is it very complicated?' asked Frankie.

'Oh, no, no, no,' beamed Miss Tatum. 'It's quite straightforward. But you do have to remember a few lines of rhyme. Don't worry, you'll pick it up in two shakes. Come with me.' She ushered Frankie into a side room and closed the door on them.

'What should we do?' Jack asked Mr Lovejoy.

'Are we going to help make Jack's costume?' asked Tom.

'No, Mr Fox is dealing with all that,' said Mr Lovejoy. 'But the May Queen's costume needs cutting up.'

'Cutting up?' Regan said, puzzled. 'Do you mean cutting *out*?'

Mr Lovejoy smiled. 'Not at all. The traditional May Queen costume is made up of red and white paper streamers. Here, I'll show you how it works.'

The makings of the costume were already to hand. It consisted of lengths of white material and piled sheets of red and white crepe paper. The sheets of paper were to be cut into narrow strips and the strips attached to the white material, which was then cut into sections to form a waistband, a shoulderband and a headband. The May Queen would tie these around herself and walk at the head of the main procession as it wove its way through the streets.

According to Mr Lovejoy, Frankie would be expected to do a lot of smiling and waving as she led the parade to a special place just outside the village. And it was there that she would speak her rhyme, after which the people would head off for the bonfire.

'Then the May Queen will be involved in one final ritual elsewhere,' said Mr Lovejoy. 'After that, the feasting can begin in earnest. It should all be tremendous fun.'

'What kind of final ritual?' asked Jack.

Mr Lovejoy gave them a mysterious smile. 'Ah!' he said. 'That would be telling. That would quite spoil the surprise!'

The side door opened and Frankie and Miss Tatum emerged. Frankie's eyebrows were lowered in concentration and she was mouthing something under her breath.

Tom saw a fleeting glance pass between Mr Lovejoy and Miss Tatum. Miss Tatum gave an almost imperceptible nod and a broad smile spread across Mr Lovejoy's face.

Frankie looked at the silver-haired, lily-frail old lady. 'I'd like to practise it a few times,' she said. 'I'm pretty sure I've got it, but I'd like to be certain.'

'Well, I'll tell you what,' said Miss Tatum. 'It looks like your costume is almost finished. Why don't the four of you go off to the Stone of Wyrd and have a proper dress rehearsal?'

'The Stone of *what*?' said Tom.

'Wyrd. I'll show it to you,' said Frankie. 'Miss Tatum has told me all about it.' She looked at the pile of stranded crepe paper. 'So? How does this cozzy work, then?'

Miss Tatum showed her how to tie the lengths of material around her waist and across her forehead, and how to loop it about her shoulders so that the red and white streamers made a rustling cloak that came almost to her feet.

'Hey, not bad,' said Regan as Frankie did a twirl in a flurry of fluttering coloured strips. 'Eat your heart out, Calvin Klein.'

'Now then,' said Miss Tatum. 'You don't want all and sundry seeing you in your regal outfit, do you? Of course not, not until tomorrow.' She explained how they could get to the Stone of Wyrd via the back ways of the village.

'That's the ticket,' said Mr Lovejoy, beaming at Frankie. 'You go off and enjoy yourselves for an hour or so, and then you can come back and help us with the rest of the preparations.'

They left the hall and made their way through the quiet lanes and alleys that meandered between the pretty cottages that slumbered in their charming, well-tended gardens.

Bodin Summerley was not a large village and, away from the high street, the houses and cottages seemed undisturbed by a century of change. The air seemed drowsy; still and unnaturally warm for so early in the year.

They came out into an open area; a wide semi-circle of tall grasses skirted by woodland. Doing her best not to get her legs tangled in the red and white ribbons of crepe paper, Frankie headed into the grass.

The Stone of Wyrd was a long regular oval of pure white stone, about two metres long and half a curved metre in height. It lay embedded in the ground, as smooth and satin-faced as a giant egg tossed down by some passing Celtic god way back in the deeps of time.

'Apparently the tradition is that the May Queen leads the people here,' explained Frankie. 'Then she climbs onto the Stone of Wyrd, recites a little poem-type thing, and then sends them off to the bonfire.' She pointed away to the left. 'Which is going to be on a hill over there somewhere behind those trees.'

'Mr Lovejoy said you'd have some other stuff to do as well,' said Tom.

Frankie nodded. 'That's right. Miss Tatum wouldn't tell me what, but she said it was really important.'

'It's probably a one-way trip to the bonfire,' said Regan.

Frankie grinned. 'Oh, no,' she said, shaking her head in a flutter of red and white strips. 'I asked her about that. The May Queen doesn't get burned at all. Jack has that pleasure all to himself.'

'Looking forward to it,' said Jack. It puzzled him a little that he had become so calm about the whole thing. A shred of memory niggled at the back of his mind, as though something was trying to tell him that he should be wary of the bonfire. But the tiny voice was very faint, and the heavy contentment that suffused his mind all but suffocated it.

'So?' said Regan. 'What's with the poem?'

'Oh, yes,' said Frankie. 'The poem. Tell you what – give me a leg up onto the stone and I'll give it a go.'

Frankie had to be careful how she mounted the slippery rock, not only for fear of losing her footing on the smooth surface, but also to avoid ripping strips out of her frail costume.

Frankie stood, legs braced, on the highest point of the oval boulder. The others stepped back. The sun burned like a raw wound in the yawning sky. A million tons of hot, dead air slumped down over the small field.

Frankie felt a bead of sweat trickle down the side of her face. She licked her upper lip and tasted salt. The fierce sunlight seemed to be acting like a prism, taking shapes and colours and splitting them, distorting them. Tom and Regan and Jack stood below her in an arc, a couple of metres away from the white rock. But they were standing at such bizarre, gravity-defying angles – leaning impossibly far back.

Frankie felt dizzy. The surface of the white stone changed beneath her feet. It rippled like water. She stretched out her arms for balance.

'Go on, then, make with the poetry, Frankie.' Regan's voice sounded as harsh as a raven's croak.

Couldn't they see how strange everything had become?

'She's forgotten it!' said Tom in a voice that barked like a dog. 'In your own time, Frankie!'

Without thought, Frankie began to speak the words.

Come, Bel of the fires, Shining One, come.
The land is silent, all other fires are cold
Till need-fire is kindled and the Green Man is called.
The May King, the Green Man, Green Georgie,
Jack, Jack, Jack-in-the-Green . . .

The huge, gaping field of the sky blanched and reeled in Jack's eyes. The sun burned, a shimmering black disk in that great stretched sheet of agonizing whiteness. The Stone of Wyrd flared like phosphorous and Frankie's form wavered and quivered as if in a heat haze.

Somewhere, terrifyingly close but infinitely far away, the air was split by the echoing whinnying of a horse and the gleeful crackle of flames. Fires rose up around the form upon the white rock.

Frankie?

A ramping horse.

A dark laughing thing crowned with antlers.

A shining golden presence that withered the world.

A voice screamed, tearing open the fabric of Jack's mind.

'Frankie! Look out!' It was Regan's voice. Screaming in shock and panic. 'Frankie – you're on fire!'

CHAPTER TWELVE
Walpurgisnacht

The day slammed back into focus, like an iron hammer striking an anvil. The hem of Frankie's paper cloak was smouldering. She stared down at the haze of thin smoke that curled up from the crackling paper. Red flames lapped, retreated, then began to grow, raging up the shrivelling threads of the cloak, leaving black flying shreds in their wake.

Frankie couldn't move. It was as if the fire was nothing to do with her. The hungry flames looked so pretty, the way they ate up the red and white and left only black flayed fibres. It seemed a shame to stop them. So pretty.

Tom reached her first. He crashed against the stone and grabbed at her. A handful of paper strips came away. Frankie tottered and slid backwards. Tom grabbed again and the burning cloak tore loose from around her shoulders as she fell.

Regan bounded around the stone. Frankie was lying spreadeagled on her back, her face quite blank. Unceremoniously, Regan ripped the waistband and headband away from Frankie and flung them into the grass.

'For heaven's *sake*, Frankie!' Regan yelled. 'Didn't you *see?*'

The remains of the cloak curled and dwindled as the flames consumed them, leaving only black strands on the white rock.

'Is she OK?' asked Jack.

Regan leaned close over her friend. 'Well?' she said. 'Are you?'

Frankie sat upright, blinking at the anxious faces of her friends. 'How did that happen?' she asked.

'I don't know,' said Jack. 'But . . . but I've been having dreams about fire for the past few days. It . . . it must have been some kind of . . . warning.'

Regan looked at him. 'Uh . . . care to run that past us again, Jack?'

'You mean you had a *premonition?*' gaped Frankie. 'You're kidding?'

'He's not kidding,' said Tom. 'Things like that do happen in our family – at least, to some of us. Mum. Gran. And Jack.'

'Hey, can you foresee exam questions?' asked Regan. 'Now, that'd be—'

'Don't be stupid,' said Jack. 'It's nothing like that. It just *happens*, sometimes. I can't control it.' He looked at Frankie. 'But the dreams must have been warning me about your costume catching fire.' He ran his fingers through his hair. 'I thought it was *me*. I thought the fire was going to happen to me. That was why I wasn't too keen on being Jack-in-the-Green.' He blew out a breath of relief. 'But it wasn't me at all. It was you.'

'I wish you'd said something,' Frankie complained as she got up. 'What's the point of having premonitions if you don't *tell* anyone about them?' She looked at the blackened remains of her flimsy cloak and finally realized the danger she'd been in. She felt sick.

'Jack doesn't like people to know about that stuff,' said Tom.

'That's right,' Jack said, frowning at Frankie and Regan. 'And it's not premonitions, it's just things that go on inside my head sometimes. And I don't want either of you telling anyone about it, OK?'

'Yeah, but—' began Regan.

'Promise!' snapped Jack. 'Promise to keep it secret, or I'll never speak to either of you again.' The vehemence in his voice took the two girls by surprise.

'Yeah . . . sure . . .' said Regan. 'No problem, Jack.'

'We're your friends,' added Frankie. 'Of course we won't tell anyone.'

Jack's face cleared. 'We'd better get back, I suppose. It looks like the May Queen is going to need a new outfit. Preferably fireproof.'

They headed back through the long grass.

'Um, excuse me,' said Tom. 'But does anyone have any theories about how Frankie's costume caught fire in the first place? Cos if they have, I'd be really interested in hearing them.'

No one spoke.

'Well, that's a rum do, and no mistake,' Mr Lovejoy said when the friends told him what had happened. 'Burst into flames, you say? Well I never.'

'It's a blessing no one was hurt,' said Miss Tatum. She gave Frankie a reassuring smile. 'I expect your shoe sparked on the stone. It'll be something silly and simple like that. You must have been frightened, though.'

'Well, not really,' admitted Frankie. 'I should have been, but I wasn't for some reason.'

'I saved her,' said Tom. 'She was just standing there like a complete *lemon*.'

'Well, no harm done, thankfully,' said Miss Tatum. 'We'll soon make you up another costume.'

'Um, I don't know . . .' Frankie said. She wasn't at all sure she still fancied being the May Queen.

Mr Lovejoy clapped his hands together. 'Tell you what,' he said, grinning like a crocodile. 'How about we all trot off to The Wicker Man and partake of another glass each of my special drink, eh? And then you can help us to finish off the street decorations! Would you like that? Of course you would! Absolutely splendid!'

'This has been one heck of a weird day,' said Regan as she flopped back on the bed. Outside the mullioned window the night was as black as deep water.

Jack was sitting cross-legged on the other bed, nodding drowsily. Tom was sprawled, half-asleep, in an upholstered armchair. Frankie was leaning against the window frame, gazing out over the rooftops of Bodin Summerley towards the purple-shaded trees that enclosed the little village like a protective wall. Protecting what, she thought abstractedly. Protecting the village from stuff outside – or protecting everywhere else from the village? She shook her head. What a peculiar idea.

She looked over her shoulder at her sleepy friends.

'Weird and exhausting,' she said in reply to Regan's comment. But why was she so exhausted? She tried to remember where the afternoon had gone.

They'd each had a glass of the peachy squash back at The Wicker Man. And then? Frankie had vague, disjointed memories of the four of them working out in the streets of the busy village, putting up more decorations, nailing garlands and wreathes of flowers to doors and fenceposts. Everyone seemed delighted to see them – especially Jack and her – *especially* when the people were told that they were to be May Queen and Jack-in-the-Green.

And then?

A meal at The Wicker Man. Mr Lovejoy had insisted. Frankie remembered talking about heading off home . . . it was getting late . . . her dad would wonder where she was. Jack and Tom said the same. Mum and Dad will worry about us if we're not home soon.

And then?

Yes . . . yes . . . Mr Lovejoy had suggested that they phone home and ask if they could stay overnight in the village . . . all four of them . . . at the pub. It would save the journey in the morning. It had seemed like a good idea, really. Frankie remembered speaking to Samantha. She remembered Samantha sounding sceptical. She remembered Mr Lovejoy taking the phone and speaking reassuringly to Samantha. Respectable establishment. A hot meal and an early night in empty guest rooms. Plenty of adults to keep an eye on them. No, no trouble at all. A pleasure.

And then?

The same for Jack and Tom. Their father had been initially unhappy about the arrangement, but Mr Lovejoy had done the business again and it had all been settled. Regan? Well, Jennie had jumped at the chance of Regan being out for the night. Regan had said she could hear the front door slam behind Jennie almost before the telephone receiver hit the cradle.

And then?

Sleepy in front of a roaring fire. Shown to their rooms. One room for the boys – one for her and Regan. Sleepiness rising, strangling all the sense out of their brains. They'd wandered into Jack and Tom's room to chat for a while, but no one seemed to be in the mood for chatting.

Sleep, yes. Chat, no. Deep sleep. So *tired.*

Frankie peeled herself away from the window frame.

'C'mon,' she said, poking Regan, who was lying sprawled on the bed with her eyes closed. 'Long day tomorrow. Bed.'

'Yurrrgh . . .' grunted Regan. 'Grrofff . . .'

Frankie tugged at her. 'Come on,' she said. 'We're only next door. Two minutes and you'll be in your own bed. Then you can—'

The ceiling light went out.

'The bulb's gone,' murmured Jack. He lifted a limp hand and waved. 'Bye-bye, bulb.'

Frankie stumbled her way to the door and opened it. Outside, the hallway was a pit of blackness. A voice was shouting from downstairs. 'It's all right, it's only a power cut. No need to panic. It happens all the time.'

'Can we have candles?' Frankie called into the blackness. There was no reply. She considered making her way downstairs in the pitch darkness, but decided against it. Oh, well, no candles, then.

A soft, familiar voice whispered in her mind. *On the eve of Beltane all fires in the village would be extinguished.*

She turned. The sky outside the window, which had seemed black before, now shone with a strange, lambent, deep blue light.

Jack was standing at the window, silhouetted against the eerie blue luminescence of the night sky. 'The whole village is blacked out,' he said. 'There isn't a single solitary light anywhere.'

'That'll mess up their festival but *good*,' murmured Regan.

'It'll be fixed by then,' mumbled Tom. 'Easy.'

Frankie made her way over to the window. A feathery radiance seemed to be hanging over the village.

She fell into a waking dream.

A drumbeat sounded from down in the street. A lone man came prancing through the night, brandishing a long ribbon-hung pole. Red and White. There was something attached to the end of the pole. Something wedge-shaped and lumpy.

There was laughter and singing. A whole troop of people came dancing through the radiant night under Frankie's dreaming gaze. Bells jingled and voices were lifted in song. Some of the people were dressed in bizarre and extraordinary costumes. There was a kind of frantic, hectic edge to the singing and the dancing that made Frankie uneasy.

Were they all people? Some of them seemed too big, too heavy – shambling and humping their way along the street like . . . like animals. Like bears and stags and wolves and boars . . . all joining in with the dance . . . all risen up onto their hind legs and dancing among the people, eyes rolling, tusks champing, antlers clashing, fangs gnashing in the darkness.

And then the man with the pole turned and

headed towards The Wicker Man. The lunatic crowd followed, yells and laughter spiking up through the beat of the solitary drum. The bells rang shrill and frantic. The song had an endless, cyclic, hypnotic melody, like the slow changing of the seasons of the world.

Frankie shrank back as the thing on the end of the pole came near, bobbing closer and closer to the window. It was brown, wrinkled and puckered like old leather. White and pale brown bones showed through. There was a pit of darkness between the crumpled eyes. The lower jaw was missing, but the upper teeth grinned a mad, crooked grin.

And then the dead eyes snapped open and a blackness poured out of them. A blackness so terrible than Frankie couldn't breathe for terror. And at the heart of the blackness a red flame danced.

CHAPTER THIRTEEN
The Hobbyhorse

*B*lackness. Seething, unquiet blackness. No flames. No acid-bright stars. No smell of crushed flowers. A different smell. Peaches. Yes . . . peaches. And voices. Two voices. Strange but familiar. Like doves murmuring in the rafters.

. . . we only need to keep them under for a few more hours and it'll all be over. You've done well. Pray that the sacrifice will be enough to undo the sacrilege.

. . . they're suspicious. They've been seeing . . . things. They told me of seeing a horse. A horse that appears and vanishes.

. . . yes, yes, the door is opened. The power is abroad. The dark, old power. It has taken the path out of the old time. It comes closer moment by moment. It is angry. Its vengeance will be a cataclysm. I told you – that man Milligan will be the ruination of us all with his infernal meddling.

. . . but will the sacrifices be enough? Will it sleep again?

. . . pray that it is so.

. . . yes, pray that it is so . . .

'Wakey-wakey! Rise and shine!' Frankie was shocked out of sleep by Mr Lovejoy's lively bellow. She forced her eyelids open. The room was full of creamy, dusty light. The door was agape and Mr Lovejoy's face hung in the gap like a ripe tomato. 'Breakfast in ten minutes! Up and at 'em, sleepyheads!'

He slammed the door and Frankie heard him go stomping along to the boys' room.

Regan was looking at her from under a hump of bedclothes. She resembled a grumpy mole.

'Hi.'

'Hello.' Frankie frowned. 'Do you remember coming to bed? I don't.'

'I remember crashing out on Tom's bed.' Regan threw the blankets off and went into a huge, elaborate stretching routine. 'I wonder if the lights have been fixed?'

Frankie reached over and flicked the switch of her bedside lamp. Blossom-soft light suffused the room.

'Yup,' said Regan. 'It's fixed. Good. I'm starved. Last one to breakfast has to eat the fried tomatoes.'

'I had a nightmare . . .' said Frankie. 'At least . . .' She frowned, trying to piece together the shrapnel of the previous evening. The memory of the wild dance was like a bruise on her mind. 'Regan – I really don't remember coming to bed!'

Regan ripped the curtains open. The sky was wonderfully blue. 'Are you in bed, or aren't you in bed?'

'Yes, I'm in bed.'

'So, you must have *come* to bed, right?'

'Ye-es . . .'

'So? What's your problem?'

Frankie shook her head. 'Oh, nothing.' She got out of bed. 'Anyway, I *like* fried tomatoes.'

'Yurrgh!'

*

Breakfast in The Wicker Man's back room was a noisy, chaotic affair, with Mr Lovejoy and various other people rushing to and fro with cereals and fry-ups and toast and jam until the four friends felt as full as balloons.

'Another glass of Mr Lovejoy's patent elixir?' The pub landlord hovered at Jack's shoulder with a jug of the pink juice and a beaming smile.

'No. Thank you,' gasped Jack, pushing his plate back. 'I couldn't manage another thing.'

'I could just go straight back to sleep,' Regan said, patting her stomach.

'I think not,' laughed Mr Lovejoy. He pointed to Frankie and Jack. 'You two are definitely needed.'

'Where do we go?' asked Frankie.

'The May Queen will be decked out in her finery by Miss Tatum in the church hall,' said Mr Lovejoy. He turned to Jack. 'And your outfit is finished and waiting for you in Mr Fox's cottage.'

'What about us?' asked Tom.

'You two might like to go with the May Queen,' said Mr Lovejoy. 'I'm sure Florella will have plans for you.' Mr Lovejoy clapped his hands. 'Now then!' he hooted. 'No time to lose, my friends. On with the motley, eh? On with the jolly old motley!'

Two minutes later the four of them were out in the open at the front of the pub. The yellow and red decorations hung limp in the still air. The sun made their eyes water. Shadows were cast as sharp as swords.

'Well,' said Jack. 'I suppose I'll catch you lot later, then.'

'I guess so,' said Regan. 'I can't wait to see your costume!'

Jack headed down the side street towards the front

of Mr Fox's cottage. He remembered dreaming a formless black dream. And voices. He remembered voices.

He walked up the winding, hedge-haunted path to Mr Fox's front door. The black iron door-knocker was in the shape of a leering face with vines for hair. Sinuous plant-tendrils slid from the corners of the wide-stretched mouth.

The door opened to a single rap of the heavy knocker.

'Jack! Excellent!' Mr Fox was dressed up in what looked to Jack like a jester's uniform, formed of red and yellow diamond-shaped patches. The disc of his face protruded from a cap with three curved points. 'What do you think of my costume? I'm The Fool.' He chuckled. 'And there's no fool like an old fool, hmm? But it's an important role. I lead Jack-in-the-Green around the bounds of the village. It's an ancient ritual. Come in, my boy. Everything's ready for you.'

'Are you feeling better?' Jack asked as he stepped over the threshold. 'And have you heard anything more about the burglar? Have they found the head at all?'

'As for myself,' said Mr Fox as he guided Jack along the cosy little hallway, 'I feel as right as rain.' He smiled. 'No sense, no feeling, so they say, hmm? But I've heard nothing about the thief. I expect the police are pursuing every avenue of enquiry. That's the phrase, isn't it? Every avenue of enquiry.' He extended a red and yellow arm. 'In here, my boy.'

Jack would never have said so, but Mr Fox's wrinkled, hawkish old face looked totally bizarre poking out from the Fool's cap. Not *funny* bizarre –

unsettling bizarre. Like a wicked old raven's head jutting from a parrot's plumage.

Jack entered Mr Fox's living room.

'There you are!' said Mr Fox. 'Jack-in-the-Green!'

Standing in the middle of the room was a large bell-shaped wickerwork frame constructed of twined branches. Flowers and leafy twigs were threaded in and out of the framework. The room smelled sick-sweet and acrid.

Jack's head spun.

The door thudded shut at his back. A key clicked in a lock.

He heard a low, throaty chuckle.

He turned as though in a dragging nightmare and saw the hideous mummified horse's head looming towards him . . .

'Whoo! That's a bit creepy!' said Regan. An extraordinary shape bobbed and swayed at the front entrance to the church hall. It was a boat-shaped frame, almost two metres tall, and covered with black cloth. Black fringes trailed on the ground as the thing rose and fell, as though tossed on an imaginary ocean. At one end was fixed a tall, stylized horse's head, painted black and hung with ribbons of yellow and red.

The contraption lumbered towards them, did a quick bow and snapped its wooden teeth together. Snap-snap.

'Uh . . . nice horsey . . .' said Regan. The wooden teeth snapped again, then the contraption turned and went snapping after a gang of small children, scattering them in giggles.

'I see you've met our Hobbyhorse,' said Miss Tatum. She was standing at the open doors to the hall. She smiled as the unwieldy, cumbersome thing chased the laughing children. As it dipped, they could see trouser legs and shoes showing under the long black fringe.

'It's our Mr Gallows, you know,' explained Miss Tatum. 'He's the blacksmith. You need a strong back to support all that woodwork.' She ushered the three friends into the busy hall. 'He'll be hungry as a hunter and dry as a bone by this evening. But there'll be food and drink for everyone, I'm sure. All those that are left.'

She turned and looked at Tom and Regan. 'Now then, what would you like to do?'

'We'll help out with anything that needs doing,' offered Tom.

'You name it,' said Regan, 'and we'll do it.'

'Well, I'm sure I'll be able to come up with something for you in a little while,' said Miss Tatum. 'But right now, I must get the May Queen sorted out. That's very important, eh, Frankie?'

'I'll say.'

'We've put a new costume together,' said Miss Tatum, stretching her arm around Frankie's shoulders. 'It's in that little back room where we went yesterday. Shall we go and try it on?' She looked at Tom and Regan. 'We won't be long.'

Miss Tatum led Frankie up along the side of the bustling hall.

Tom and Regan looked at one another.

'Well?' asked Regan. 'Any brilliant plans?'

'If no one needs us here,' said Tom, 'I'd quite like to go and take a look at the bonfire.'

Regan nodded. 'Yeah, that sounds fine. Do you know where it is exactly?'

'Nope, but we can ask.'

They soon found out how to get to Mummers Hill – the site of the May Day bonfire. The hill, they were told, was just outside the village bounds, and the quickest way to get there would be down past the church hall, through the churchyard and straight along the old lanes out of the village.

Everything went smoothly until they came out of the serene churchyard and entered the first of the narrow lanes. That was when things started to go a bit haywire.

'Awww – *what*?' exclaimed Regan as they came to the third dead end. Tom shrugged and turned on his heel. These old back lanes out of the village were more complicated than he'd expected. The lanes were bounded by stone walls or thick bushes or tall wooden fences; it was almost like they'd been designed as a maze.

Or perhaps the lanes were deliberately bending back upon themselves to prevent the two friends from getting out of the village? The heavy, suffocating atmosphere in the deserted old pathways was so charged that almost anything was believable.

A large black shape glided across the end of the lane.

'Hey!' said Regan. 'That's the Hobbyhorse guy. Tom – give him a yell. He'll know the way out.'

Tom ran to the end of the alley. 'Mr Gallows! Mr Gallows! Stop!' The bulky black shape bobbed into another of the lanes. 'Oh, rats! He didn't hear me!'

He raced after the Hobbyhorse. He came to a skidding halt at the mouth of the alleyway. The lane wound into thick overgrown greenery. Puzzled, Tom called out again. Mr Gallows must have moved like lightning to be out of sight already.

Regan caught up with him.

'Well?'

'Down here.'

They rounded a dogleg bend and were confronted by a moss-grown wall of dull brown stone.

'Another dead end!' raved Regan. 'Who designed this darned town – Marvin the Magician?'

A sharp snapping noise cracked the air at their backs.

They turned. The Hobbyhorse filled the lane behind them. It moved slowly, as if on a rippling sea. The head dipped and the painted eyes stared at them.

'Mr Gallows!' Tom gasped with laughter. 'Nice trick! Where were you hiding?' The Hobbyhorse seemed to have materialized out of thin air. 'Can you tell us the way out of here? We're totally lost.'

The huge black shape swayed. The wooden teeth clicked together.

'Uh . . . Mr Gallows . . . ?' said Regan. 'This is amazingly funny, and all that, but we'd really like to get out of here, if that's OK with you.' She marched determinedly towards the Hobbyhorse. 'Like, *now*, please?'

The great black frame reared up over Regan, the hanging fringes rising up off the ground.

'Regan! Careful!' But Tom's warning came a second too late. The leading edge of the plunging frame struck Regan's shoulder and she fell with a cry of pain.

'*Regan!*' Tom ran forwards as the front of the Hobbyhorse dropped and Regan was engulfed.

'Leave her alone!' Tom yelled, beating at the black cloth with both hands. 'Get off! You're hurting her!'

The big teeth snapped close to his ear and the Hobbyhorse reared once more. Tom lashed out blindly. His forearm struck across the thing's neck and it slumped to one side like a collapsing mountain.

Regan was face-down on the ground. Tom hooked his hand under her arm and dragged her to her feet. He couldn't even begin to think about what was happening. Had Mr Gallows gone crazy?

Regan blinked at him. Momentarily disorientated.

The Hobbyhorse gathered itself and rose above them like a black cloud.

'Run!' screamed Regan.

Tom didn't need telling twice – the expression on her face was enough.

They pelted back along the alley.

'We have to get help,' Regan panted as they fled. 'Find someone. Anyone. This is too weird.' She threw Tom a frightened glance. 'There was no-one under there, Tom.'

'What?'

'Honest-to-gosh!' gasped Regan. 'There wasn't a *person* under there. There was just . . . like . . . *nothing*! Nothing at all!'

CHAPTER FOURTEEN
Jack-in-the-Green

Regan and Tom ran wildly. Bitter-smelling ivy snatched at their shoulders, roses flung out thorny tendrils to trip them. Walls loomed up suddenly in their faces, forcing them to wheel around and race back the way they had come. And at every bend and turn in the endless, formless alleyways they feared to encounter the great black menace of the Hobbyhorse.

They dashed around another corner.

'Good heavens! What's this!' They cannoned into the solid, sturdy, *human* shape of Mr Lovejoy, almost knocking him off his feet.

Tom had no idea how they'd got there, but they were at the rear of the church hall.

'Back ... there ...' Regan spluttered, pointing frantically the way they had come, '... thing ... a thing ... not joking ... hit me ... nothing ... *nothing there!*'

Mr Lovejoy's broad arms swept around them. 'Be still!' he said in a commanding tone that they had not heard before. 'You're not making sense! What have you seen?'

Tom took a deep breath, his heart pounding like timpani in his chest. 'We saw the Hobbyhorse,' he managed to gasp. 'It attacked us.'

'There was no one in it!' shouted Regan. 'It was moving – *on its own!*'

Mr Lovejoy stared over their heads. 'So,' he muttered. 'It has begun.' Powerful hands clamped down on Tom and Regan's shoulders. 'Let's hope the sacrifice will be enough.' His fingers dug into their flesh. 'If not, others may be needed.'

Tom stared up at him. There was an uncanny light in Mr Lovejoy's eyes.

Mr Lovejoy looked down at them. 'Don't be afraid,' he said. 'The power is running on apace, but it isn't here yet. Not altogether. Trust me and I'll protect you. Say nothing! Come with me!'

He hardly needed to have given his final command. The two friends had little choice but to go with him; his hands were like steel clamps on their shoulders.

He led them across the road to The Wicker Man. A few people glanced at them, but no one intervened.

Mr Lovejoy pushed them into the hot gloom of the public house. He thrust them along a corridor, not giving them time to gather their wits or draw breath. He opened a door.

'In here,' he said. 'You'll be safe down there. I'll do what I can to help your friends.'

Regan stumbled into darkness and almost fell headlong down a flight of rough stairs.

'Wait!' panted Tom. 'What are you doing?' But the big man pushed him in after Regan and slammed the door on the two of them. Tom heard a bolt bang home.

Absolute, pitchy blackness engulfed them.

Regan's voice wavered out of the blind dark.

'Tom?'

'Yes.'

'I think we're in big trouble. What do you think?'

'It will be worth it,' Mr Fox said as he slowly circled the wickerwork frame. He tucked a loose, leafy off-shoot into place and leaned forward to peer at Jack through the latticework of twigs. 'I know it's a lot to ask of you, but it's the only way.'

Jack's mouth was bone dry. He couldn't remember getting unto the wickerwork frame. His head swam. He remembered the mummified horse's head looming in his face, and then a gulping, absorbing oblivion had taken him.

'The head was never stolen, was it?' Jack managed to say, cotton-mouthed.

'No, it never was.' Mr Fox's voice had an incongruous, sing-song quality to it. 'I hid it away, away, away.' He looked at Jack with crow-bright eyes. 'I hit myself on the head, you know. Painful. And very difficult to do.' He hummed to himself for a few moments. 'But it had to be done. I had to convince everyone that the head was gone.'

'What's ... going ... to happen ... to ... me ... ?'

Mr Fox cocked his bird-head and the absurd red and yellow points of his cap flopped forwards. 'You'll be led around the old boundary-markers of the village,' said Mr Fox. 'It's called *Beating the Bounds*. And then you'll be taken to the bonfire – to the Beltane fire.' He frowned. 'It isn't our fault, you know. None of this is our fault. If that stupid man had left well alone ...' He stopped and a discordant grin cracked across his face. '*Well* alone,' he cackled. 'Did you hear what I said? If he'd left the well *well* alone.'

'I don't understand,' said Jack. His head was muzzy and the smell from the frame was sickening. 'Who are you talking about?'

'Your friend,' muttered Mr Fox. 'Milligan. The archaeologist. I tried to stop him digging, but he wouldn't be told.' Mr Fox's face came right up close to the wickerwork so that Jack was staring straight into the feral eyes. 'The head should never have been disturbed,' he said. 'If you give a gift to a god, you can't just dig it up and snatch it back when it suits you.' The tone of Mr Fox's voice changed, as though he was trying to explain a simple fact to a fool. 'That makes the god angry, you see? You do see, don't you? And there's only one tried and true method of appeasing an angry god.' Mr Fox made a clicking noise with his tongue as he spotted a twig out of place on the bell-shaped frame. He patted it into position.

He stepped back. 'There now, all done!' His eyebrows lowered. 'Now, you *will* co-operate, won't you? The sacrifice must be made.' Mr Fox lifted his arm and Jack saw the glint of a curiously shaped knife-blade in his fist. Mr Fox toyed with the knife, angling it until a flash of sunlight from the window hit across Jack's eyes.

Jack tried to turn away. It was then that he realized that he was bound fast inside the frame. His arms were pinned at his sides. Hoops of wickerwork held his shoulders, chest and waist.

Mr Fox brought the flashing knife closer to Jack's face. 'You really must reconcile yourself to the fact that the sacrifice will happen. The proper place is in the Beltane fire.' Sunlight flared brightly in Jack's eyes as the blade twisted. 'But it isn't so terribly important that you die in the fire – so long as the god gets his blood. So long as his anger is soothed and the village is saved.'

Jack understood what the crazy old man meant: either walk voluntarily into the flames, or die here.

'So?' said Mr Fox. 'What's it to be, my boy?'

Jack swallowed hard. 'Just tell me what to do,' he croaked from a desert throat. It was the only way to free himself from this nightmare. If he could just get out of the madman's cottage, he would be able to raise the alarm – to shout for help.

Once the people realized what was really going on at this terrible festival, they would put a stop to it. They would save him.

After all – the entire *village* couldn't have gone insane.

'Pretty as a picture!' Miss Tatum cooed. She gently patted Frankie's cheeks. 'I swear you'll be the most beautiful May Queen in the entire country.'

They were in the little back room in the church hall. Frankie eyed herself in a full-length mirror that was propped against one wall. The May Queen costume was similar to the one which had been destroyed, except that some shiny red and yellow ribbon had been found to make up the cascade of rippling strips.

The effect was quite different. The old paper costume had been light and fluttery, like moth wings. When Frankie swung her hips now, the new ribbons moved in a graceful wave of reflected light.

Red and yellow ribbons winked among her long

golden hair. She practised smiling and waving. The cloak spread from her raised arm, sparking light, like the wing of some fantastic, mythical bird.

Behind her, reflected in the mirror, Frankie saw Miss Tatum's face.

She snapped her head around in shock.

But the horrible, starved expression wasn't there. Miss Tatum smiled at her as serenely and gently as ever.

Frankie giggled nervously.

'Pretty as a picture,' sighed Miss Tatum, her hands clasped at her throat.

Frankie let the ribbons flow over her hand. 'Let's hope it doesn't catch fire,' she said with a slightly forced laugh.

'Oh, no, that would never do,' said Miss Tatum. 'It's Jack who burns. The May Queen is sacrificed in quite another way.'

Frankie looked at her. 'Is that the secret you wouldn't tell me yesterday?' she said. 'The final ritual?'

'It is,' said Miss Tatum. Her face became almost melancholy. 'We wouldn't want to burn a pretty thing like you, my dear.'

Frankie laughed. 'That's good news,' she said. 'So? How do I die?'

'Well, I don't suppose it'll do any harm to tell you, now. It's too late for . . .' She paused, as if reconsidering her words. 'It'll all be over soon, anyway.' Miss Tatum moved close to Frankie and slid an arm around her shoulders. The ribbons rustled.

'After you speak the words on the Stone of Wyrd,' the old lady hissed into Frankie's ear, 'we will take you to a special place. A very special place. In the woods. A small glade. A very, very old glade. The druids once worshipped there, and the land doesn't forget. People forget, but the land doesn't. The earth has a great appetite for blood, my dear.' The arm squeezed around Frankie's shoulders. 'Just think of it, Frankie. Think of all the centuries, of all the May Queens who have walked exactly the same path through the forest.'

Frankie swallowed, wanting to be free of the old lady's embrace. 'What happens in the glade?' she whispered.

'You will be bound with your face against the sacred oak.' Miss Tatum's voice was as sibilant as a snake. 'And then the words will be spoken over you, and the knife plunged into your back.'

Frankie twisted out from under Miss Tatum's arm, alarm showing on her face.

'Oh, my dear, I've frightened you, I'm so sorry,' said Miss Tatum. She shook her head. 'I am an old tattle-tale, aren't I? I can never hold my tongue. But don't worry, it'll be over very quickly.'

'This is all pretence – right?' said Frankie. 'The May Queen isn't killed. Not really. You said – you told me – *you* were the May Queen once . . . so . . . it's just make-believe, isn't it?'

'Yes, yes, I was,' Miss Tatum sighed wistfully. 'Many, many years ago, in a costume made of dyed silk. I still remember it. But the old power was asleep then.' A light ignited behind the old lady's eyes. 'He should never have been disturbed. Let sleeping dogs lie, I say. Let the bygone things stay buried.'

'You're talking about the shaft, aren't you?' said Frankie. 'You're talking about that mummified horse's head.'

'People dig and grub and grovel in the earth,' hissed Miss Tatum. 'They don't give a thought to whose peace they disturb.' Her eyes flashed. 'Things buried deep should be left to sleep. It's an act of madness to wake him up – and after all this *time*.'

The old lady glided to a small table that stood at one side of the room. Frankie had noticed the ornate box that rested on the table top, but hadn't paid it much attention. Miss Tatum opened the lid and took out a long knife with a curved, leaf-shaped blade.

'And isn't it always the way?' she said as she moved towards Frankie. 'That the rest of us are left to clear up the mess caused by others?' She smiled like a serpent. 'But don't you worry, my dear, it'll all be over by teatime.'

Frankie dived for the door that led back out to the stage.

She couldn't believe this was really happening – but she knew one thing for sure: she wanted nothing more to do with the festival. She wanted to get as far away from this place as possible, even if it meant running all the way home with the red and yellow ribbons streaming out behind her.

She jerked the door open. A large shape filled the frame.

Frankie jumped back, startled. 'Oh!' she gasped in relief. 'Mr Lovejoy! Thank heavens!'

Mr Lovejoy moved into the room and closed the door firmly behind himself. He glanced at the knife in Miss Tatum's hand.

'Well, now, Florella,' he said levelly. 'This is all a bit *previous*, isn't it?' He stepped forwards and snatched hold of Frankie. He spun her, clamping an arm around her neck, crushing her against his side.

'Now then, what have you two been talking

about?' he said as Frankie struggled desperately in his grip. 'I mean to say, what on earth have you been telling the poor girl, Florella?'

CHAPTER FIFTEEN
The Fires of Bel

Jack, Jack, Jack-in-the-Green
Green Jack we attend
Feed our herds well, Jack
Make fruitful our crops
To the fire, to the fire,
To the fire we take you
Jack, Jack, Jack-in-the-Green!

The world spun like a Catherine wheel; like a wild kaleidoscope. Through the bars of his wickerwork prison-cage, Jack watched in a daze as shapes and colours exploded and collided and whirled and danced.

It had started the moment the procession had reached the first boundary stone. Sweat ran freely down Jack's face and neck, but the gag that Mr Fox had bound across his mouth made it impossible for him to cry out and alert anyone to his peril.

The Fool brought a stick down on the stone and everyone cheered. No one paid any attention to the heavy, lumpy bundle of cloth that he carried under his arm.

If Jack faltered, a dozen hands helped push him on his way; a couple of dozen voices shouted and sang and laughed.

It was all part of the festivities; all part of the ceremony.

And then, as though his senses had overloaded, the mad whirl shuddered to a halt and Jack stared through the wicker at a steady but unfamiliar scene.

He was standing alongside a rough wicker fence which stretched in a long, uneven ring around a broad area of earth and trampled grass. Within the wicker stockade squatted several buildings: big, round buildings with mud walls and conical thatched roofs. He could hear the bleat of sheep and goats, and the contented grunting of rooting pigs.

A gate was open in the fence and a procession of people was passing out of the stockade. They made their way over an earth causeway that bridged a deep ditch. The ditch ran right around the stockade.

The sky was steel-grey and a fine chilling drizzle was falling. The people were clad in woollen clothing: long dresses, tunics and baggy trousers, dyed in basic, primary colours: blue, green, red, yellow. Red and yellow.

At the head of the procession a tall figure strode, dressed in a long white robe. From his forehead, antlers clawed at the rain-soaked sky like crippled fingers.

Jack watched as the procession wound its way in under the sodden eaves of the forest. Then his eyes were drawn back to the stockade. A pole thrust up from among the buildings, maybe six or seven metres in height. Something was attached to the pole, right up near the top. Jack screwed his eyes against the chilling rain-flurries. The thing swam into focus. It was the skull of a cow. The huge, hollow eye-sockets stared out impassively over the forest.

Jack heard a horse whinnying in the distance. He turned to pinpoint the source of the sound and the world erupted around him once again into multi-coloured chaos.

It hadn't taken Tom long to find the light switch. At least now they knew where they were. The walls of the pub cellar were a dull, dingy white. Crates of bottles were stacked here and there, along with beer barrels and other boxes. A long wooden chute led up to a trapdoor, but the angle was too steep for them to climb, even with Regan on Tom's shoulders.

Regan used up a lot of useless energy hammering on the locked door at the head of the stairs. There was no sound of movement in the pub.

'You're wasting your time,' Tom told her. 'Everyone will be at the festival. There's no one out there. Trust me.'

Regan sat disconsolately at the foot of the stairs with her chin in her hands.

'What the heck is going on in this crazy mixed-up town?' she said. 'I feel like I've walked in halfway through a spooky film and no one will tell me the plot.'

'It *is* spooky,' said Tom. He gnawed his lower lip. 'It's *very* spooky. Did you hear what Mr Lovejoy said when we told him about the Hobbyhorse-thing? He said: *It has begun. Let's hope the sacrifice will be enough. If not, others may be needed.*'

'Yeah, right,' said Regan. 'And that makes a whole lot of sense, I don't think.'

Tom looked at her. 'I've got a photographic

memory for things like that. I remember his exact words. After he'd said that stuff about the sacrifice, he said: *The power is running on apace, but it isn't here yet.*' He licked his dry lips. 'I think he was talking about something that he was really scared of, you know? Some bad . . . thing.'

Regan stared at him. 'Bad?' she repeated. 'You mean, like . . . uh . . . a *supernatural* kind of bad thing? Like a ghost or whatever?' She frowned. 'Well, isn't that exactly what I've been saying all along? I said that horse was a ghost horse and no one would listen to me.' She looked around her. 'Well, this is a fine time to be proven right!'

'Jack believed you,' said Tom. 'Don't you remember? He thought it was something to do with that horse's head that got dug up.'

Regan's eyes widened. 'Hey! That's right! We were just talking about that when . . .' She paused, eyebrows lowered. 'When *what*, Tom? It's all kind of hazy after that.'

'I'm not sure,' said Tom. 'But I remember wanting to go home. And then all of a sudden I didn't want to any more. But I can't remember why. Regan? I know it sounds totally barmy, but I've got a really bad feeling about this festival. I think Jack and Frankie are in danger. I think something has been . . . I don't know . . . let *out* of that old well. Something that was bottled up down there.'

Regan shivered and wrapped her arms around herself. 'You mean something nasty has gotten loose?' She said. 'And those guys up there – Mr Lovejoy and his pals – they plan on whacking Frankie and Jack – using them as sacrifices to try and convince the *whatever-it-is* to go bye-byes in the well again?'

'It can't be,' said Tom after a long, uneasy silence. 'It's totally ridiculous.'

'Yeah, totally!'

'You'd have to be potty to believe something like that!'

'Yeah!'

They stared at each other for a few moments.

'Regan, we've got to get out of here.'

'Fine. If you have some way of tunnelling through solid walls, I'll be right behind you, man,' said Regan. 'I mean, check this place out.' She scanned the dull white walls. 'A person would need a . . . bulldozer . . . to . . . get . . .' She stood up and walked towards the far wall, her eyes fixed on something that Tom couldn't see. '. . . out . . . of . . . here . . . oh, wow!'

'What?'

'Look!'

Tom ran over to where she was standing. At a distance, he had taken it for a shadow or a chuck knocked out of the paintwork, but close up he could see exactly what had made Regan go *wow!*

A lump was missing out of the wall. Clods of earth and pieces of brick were scattered on the floor. Regan stretched her arm into the hole. Her groping hand met empty air.

She looked around, her blue eyes shining. 'I know what this is,' she breathed. 'When you let the ladder down the well to get me out, it knocked a hole in the side. In the side where the pub is!' She scrabbled frantically at the hole, wrenching out more bricks.

Tom searched for a tool. He found a rusty old crowbar and soon the two of them were working furiously at the hole, clawing and hacking away at the edges until enough bricks and plaster and earth had been dug away for Regan to get her shoulders through.

She pulled back, smeared with mud but grinning. 'Someone's put the tarp back,' she said, 'but the ladder's still there!' She let out a bark of exultant laughter. 'Tommy-boy! We're out of here!'

'Let go of me!' Frankie screamed, writhing like an eel in the lock of Mr Lovejoy's powerful arm.

'Be still!' shouted Mr Lovejoy, shaking Frankie until her teeth rattled. 'Be still, or, by the powers, I'll finish this thing right now!'

Frankie caught her breath and stopped struggling.

'Look,' she gasped, 'I don't know ... what you people ...' She gulped past iron muscles. 'I don't know what you think ... this will ... achieve ... but, please, you've got to listen to me. I don't know what's wrong, but killing Jack and me won't put it right.'

'Allow us to beg to differ,' said Mr Lovejoy. He glared daggers at Miss Tatum. 'You're a fool!' he snapped. 'You were told not to say anything. Now look at the problems you've landed us with. How are we going to get her to the temple-grove in this state?'

Miss Tatum looked crestfallen. The knife drooped in her hand.

'Well?' snarled Mr Lovejoy. 'Do you want to explain this mess to Godfrey, because I'm damned if I will.' His voice shook. 'Your tongue will be the ruin of us all, woman! Don't you realize the extent of the power that has been unleashed out there?'

'Yes. Yes, of course I do,' muttered the old lady. 'I understood every word of what Godfrey told us: we must make the blood sacrifices, just like our ancestors did in the wild times.'

'This thing has to be done in the right way,' said Mr Lovejoy. 'According to the ancient rituals.' His voice seemed suddenly to become deeper and stronger, reverberating through Frankie's body like thunder. 'The Beltane sacrifices must be offered. The alternative will see us all destroyed. If we don't appease the power it will sweep us away like chaff in the wind.'

Miss Tatum's lily-white face lifted and she looked into Frankie's eyes. 'We could kill her here,' she said. 'Right here and now.' She lifted the knife.

'No . . .' Frankie choked.

'This isn't the proper place,' said Mr Lovejoy.

'It's better than nothing,' said Miss Tatum. She advanced on Frankie, the knife raised high in her fist. 'Turn her around. The knife has to go into her back.'

'Maybe so, maybe so,' muttered Mr Lovejoy. 'Best of a bad job, eh?'

As he tried to bring Frankie's back towards the dreadful weapon, Mr Lovejoy had briefly to relax the pressure around her neck. She didn't waste the moment.

She raked the edge of her shoe down his shin and stamped on his instep with all her weight, ducking down out of the ring of his arm at the same moment.

He bellowed in pain. Frankie sidestepped Miss Tatum and ran for her one hope of escape. The door into the main body of the hall was blocked off by Mr Lovejoy, but there was a second door in the far wall of the room. She hoped desperately that it led to the outside.

She yanked it open and almost sobbed with despair as she saw that the door led to a narrow corridor and a flight of stairs. There was no exit from the building this way. But it was still better than the alternative. She dived through the door and snatched it closed in Miss Tatum's face. She heard the dull impact of the knife on the panels.

The door couldn't be locked. Frankie released the handle and scrambled up the stairs. There was a tiny landing and a door to one side. She shouldered the door open. The room beyond was some kind of attic-space under the slopes of the roof. It was filled with dusty, circling sunlit air.

She saw a small, low gable window in the back wall. Maybe it would just be big enough for her to climb through. She leaped across the room and struggled with the window latch. She heard a noise behind her. She glanced apprehensively around. Mr Lovejoy was standing in the doorway, his face a mask of seething rage. He had the knife in one bunched fist.

Frankie gave the latch a last wrench and pulled hard. The window sprang open. She plunged forwards. Her shoulders just cleared the sides of the narrow slot. She stared down at the long drop to the ground. Head first? She'd kill herself. But what other choice was there? It was the fall or the knife.

She summoned all her courage and wriggled forwards. And then a hand came down on her ankle like a vice and she was dragged backwards, kicking and fighting, into the room.

Mummers Hill was a slope of rough grass that rose in long, sweeping stages between banks of hedge and bunched copses of dark oaks, its upper edge as sharp as a wheel-rim against the blue sky. On the knees of one of the lower terraces, the black hulk of the bonfire brooded like a hunched, bent-backed monster.

Waves of nausea beat through Jack's body as the caterwauling crowd pushed him up the slope. Sweat poured off him. The sun was as hot as white iron on his face.

> *. . . To the fire, to the fire,*
> *To the fire we take you,*
> *Jack, Jack, Jack-in-the-Green!*

The smell of blossom and bitter leaves made him retch behind the gag. His feet caught in the grass but he was never allowed to fall. Up ahead The Fool was prancing towards the unlit bonfire, dancing like a lunatic marionette. Jack wondered that the old man had so much strength in his scarecrow body.

This is where they'll let me out, thought Jack. *This is where the nightmare will end.*

He was wrong. The laughing throng swept him up towards the bonfire like flotsam on a rising tide.

The Fool was dwarfed by the giant bonfire stack. He turned and held his arms up. But the crowd wasn't in the mood to quieten down. Young children ran about underfoot, playing tag and chase. People chatted and laughed and elbowed one another. Jack felt himself jostled and someone threw a stone which rattled off the back of the wicker frame.

'Karen – stop that.' A mother's voice. 'Naughty girl!'

'Get on with it!' A youth's voice from the back of the crowd. 'What's the matter, mate? Forgotten to bring the matches?'

There was laughter and applause and more shouting. Whatever The Fool had intended for this moment, the crowd wasn't prepared to tolerate speeches or long-winded rituals. The crowd wanted some action. They wanted to see the fire lit.

The Fool bounded down the hill towards where Jack was being held. Long, skeletal fingers hooked into the frame and Jack was dragged up the last few metres of the slope towards the bonfire.

The Fool's face was streaked with grime and sweat, the flesh ashen-grey and the eyes feverish. But he still had the strength to pull Jack-in-the-Green up past the bulk of the bonfire. A black post pointed up out of the crown of heaped wood.

The Fool towed Jack around to the back of the bonfire. A path of planks had been laid where the bonfire leaned back into the slope of the hill. The Fool pulled Jack along the plank-bridge towards the standing post.

There were renewed cheers from the crowd as Jack-in-the-Green and The Fool appeared on top of the bonfire heap. The Fool cavorted around the post and waved extravagantly at the people ranged on the lower slope of the hill.

Jack had been trying to marshal his remaining strength for one last great effort. He drew in a deep breath and strained at the wicker straps that held him.

Mocking laughter was his only reward. The Fool was staring in through the grill of branches, his mouth hanging open, drool on his loose lips as the gusts of laughter hacked up out of the thin throat.

The Fool was insane.

Jack was pushed up against the post and bound around and around with rope as The Fool danced in a hectic ring on the crest of the bonfire. Then

The Fool pulled the bundle from under his arm and unwrapped it.

The Fool showed the hideous head to Jack.

And then Jack was alone with his fear. The Fool was gone.

Jack saw him again, moments later, at the foot of the bonfire, still clutching the head. A few people came near him but quickly backed off again.

Some people had the feeling that Mr Fox was getting a little too deeply into his festival character. The Fool? The raving loony, more like! And what on earth was that gruesome thing he was brandishing in the face of anyone who came close? Ugh! It looked like something the cat would be ashamed to drag in. It was some nasty, putrid old horse head. Disgusting!

After all, the whole point of all that dressing up and play-acting was to have a bit of fun – not to gross everyone out. Of course, the whole sacrifice trick had to be presented convincingly: it had to look like the boy was still up there on the bonfire – even though everyone knew he'd secretly slipped out through a hatch in the back of the wicker frame.

But it had been done very well. Real sleight-of-hand stuff. There was no sign of the boy. Very clever. Great show! If you didn't know better, you could think he was still perched up there. Ha, ha, ha! But it wasn't as if anyone was really going to get barbecued that afternoon! Not really!

The Fool crouched by a pile of dry twigs. He pulled out a box of matches. Seconds later, the twigs crackled with flame. The Fool dipped a faggot in the fire, its ends bound together with pitch-smeared rags. Especially prepared and ready for him to use. A flower of flame sprang up.

For a moment, The Fool held the flaming brand aloft, then he turned and pushed it into the bonfire.

There was an expectant hush. Sweat trickled into Jack's eyes and he shook his head to try and clear his sight. For the space of twenty heartbeats nothing happened. Then a tongue of fire lapped out of the woodpile and the people cheered and whistled their approval.

A gout of white smoke rose into the air between Jack and his audience. He could still just make out the emaciated shape of The Fool through the thick fumes.

Jack watched in horror as The Fool twisted to look up at him. He lifted the horse's head towards Jack in both hands, as if it were a trophy.

The Fool started to laugh.

At that moment the day turned.

A wind sprang from nowhere and the smoke began to billow and spread until all that Jack could see through an ocean of boiling whiteness was the mummified head, hanging disembodied in the air.

A snake of smoke curled up the side of the bonfire and coiled in through the bars of the wicker frame, stinging Jack's eyes and filling his nostrils.

He heard the crowd singing:

> . . . *To the fire, to the fire,*
> *To the fire we take you*
> *Jack, Jack, Jack-in-the-Green!*

'Now what?' said Tom.

'Now we find someone who isn't totally crazy,' said

Regan. 'And we tell them what's going on around here!'

They had dragged themselves out from under the tarpaulin that covered the well and were standing uncertainly at the back of The Wicker Man.

'Fine,' said Tom. 'Great. So, tell me: who do we trust?'

Regan looked at him. 'Oh! Right!' She curled her lip. 'You mean there might be more people in on this than just Lovejoy and his pals? *Heck*, I hadn't thought of that.' She snapped her fingers. 'Got it! We find a phone, of course! Even if this entire town has gone *postal*, a call to the cops will do the biz! Tom, we gotta find a phone.'

Regan ran to the side of the building and peered cautiously around the edge. There were a few people on the high street, some carrying balloons and wearing yellow and red paper hats. They all seemed to be heading in the same direction. In the distance, she could hear brass band music. It all seemed very jolly and harmless. There was even an ice-cream van parked nearby, trailing a tail of small children.

'I haven't seen any public phones around here,' said Tom, right behind her. 'Do you think there'll be a phone in the pub?'

'Do you wanna risk that?' said Regan. 'What if Lovejoy's still hanging out in there?'

'Then we run.'

'OK. Let's go for it.'

They crept along the wall of the pub until they came to a side entrance. The door was open. Regan gave the thumbs-up sign and slid in through the doorway. Tom was at her heels and almost through the dark entrance when something made him stop and look over his shoulder.

Beyond the rooftops of Bodin Summerley, he saw a bloom of white smoke rise into the sky.

'Regan!' he hissed. 'We've got to get a move on! I think they've lit the bonfire.' He turned. The corridor forked off to the left. Regan had run out of sight around the corner. Tom followed. Regan was standing stock-still just around the bend, as if she'd been turned to stone.

Just ahead of her the terrifying black shape of the Hobbyhorse filled the corridor, undulating slowly on the swells of its invisible ocean. The black horse's head scraped the ceiling. The black fringe hung clear of the carpet. There was nothing underneath.

The big wooden teeth clacked together.

Regan's head turned slowly. 'Back off,' she breathed out of the corner of her mouth.

Tom edged away. *Bang!* The loud noise frightened the life out of him. The outer door had swung shut. *Thwack!* The heavy bolt shot home.

The Hobbyhorse surged forwards, teeth snapping.

The two friends backed away down the corridor until Tom was brought to a sudden halt by the closed door.

He scrabbled blindly for the bolt.

'Now would be a good time to get us out of here,' breathed Regan, stepping on Tom's feet as the monster bore down on them.

The bolt wouldn't move.

Whatever force had closed the door, Tom was powerless to do anything about it.

The Hobbyhorse reared up over them. Regan screamed and covered her eyes. Tom found himself staring up under the fluttering fringes of the huge creature. Red and black madness seethed and boiled.

Tom threw his arms up to protect his face as the Hobbyhorse came down over them like a black avalanche and blotted out the world.

Jack's eyes stung. The smoke was everywhere. Plumes of it gushed up into the sky. Dense white limbs of smoke scrolled along the grass. Invisible to Jack, the crowds were backing away from the bonfire, coughing and choking. The sudden squalling wind had ruined everything. The people stumbled down the hillside, grabbing their children, rubbing at their streaming eyes, tripping over one another.

Jack could hear a crackling sound, like twigs being broken and broken again. It was the sound of the fire taking hold.

It seemed futile to struggle.

Below him the triumphant mummified head rode buoyantly on the white clouds.

Jack heard a wild neighing.

A corkscrew of cloud wound around him.

He heard hoofbeats.

And then the floating head fell forwards and vanished as though finally sucked in under the billows of smoke.

He heard a solitary voice cry out.

The crackling of the flames rose up and consumed every other sound.

Panic and desperation gave Frankie the strength to break free of Mr Lovejoy's grip. Her fingers clawed over the windowsill and she shoved herself forwards. Her shins scraped over the sill and the panorama of the long fall wheeled across her eyes.

Almost instinctively, Frankie tucked her head in and swung her legs. The world spun. She bent her knees, bracing herself as best she could for the impact. The ground sloped away from the back wall of the hall. Frankie landed hard, her knees absorbing much of the shock as she rolled and skidded down the grassy bank.

She didn't pause to look back. She picked herself up and ran like the wind. The cloak of coloured ribbons had come detached at some stage, but the skirt and headband were still in place. Red and yellow strips flowed behind her.

She ran like a gale across the mown lawns of the churchyard. She half-heard a shout of rage behind her, blown away on the wind.

The day had turned. A high wind was gusting through the streets, sweeping away the thick, heavy, sorcerous air that had been suffocating the village. A cool, refreshing wind with spring flowers on its breath.

Frankie raced through the lanes as though mounted on a horse of air. The double-backs and dead-ends that had confounded Tom and Regan seemed to open up to her like the parting waves of a friendly sea.

She saw white smoke rising on a naked green hillside. People were swarming towards her, running to escape the choking billows that came rolling down the hill.

A veil of smoke drew aside, and Frankie saw a wicker shape on top of a hillock of brushwood.

'Jack!'

The crowds were too intent on getting clear of the fumes to pay any attention to Frankie as she ran up the hill towards the bonfire.

A spider-thin figure loomed out of the opaque smoke. It was silhouetted against raging red and yellow flames. It stood on the very brink of the fire, as though unaffected by the heat. It was dressed in a costume of red and yellow diamonds. It held a wedge-shaped object high in the air. It was mumbling to itself.

'Jack, Jack, Jack-in-the-Green. Green Jack we attend—' The words were broken by a bout of coughing. Shuddering breaths were taken, and the voice resumed the chant. 'Feed our herds well, Jack, make fruitful our crops.' More wracking coughs. 'To the fire, to the fire, to the fire we take you, Jack, Jack, Jack-in-the-Green.'

'Mr Fox!' Frankie narrowed her eyes against the smoke. She had recognized the cracked voice despite the bizarre costume. And she had recognized the thing that the old man held aloft. It was the mummified horse's head that was supposed to have been stolen.

The old man turned, his face contorted by some inner turmoil. His eyes widened and his jaw fell slack. The head fell out of his hands and rolled into the flames.

Mr Fox twisted as he lost grip on the precious trophy. He let out a shout of horror as he saw the flames lick greedily up around it.

The shout trailed off. A skeletal hand clutched at the narrow chest. The thin body crumpled and fell.

Frankie bounded forwards. She grabbed the old man's wrists and pulled him away from the searing heat. He lay very still. She knelt at his side, unsure of what to do.

And then she remembered Jack.

Tom wasn't going to give in without a fight. The thought of what might be happening to his brother gave him all the reason he needed to fight like a fury.

'Get off me! Get off!' Tom howled as the Hobbyhorse bore him and Regan to the floor. He had his eyes closed, but he could still see the swirling black and red that filled the hollow belly of the terrible thing. He was crushed to the carpet, but he carried on kicking and punching at the nothingness that enveloped them.

'Way to go, Tom!' Regan's voice came out of the gloom, fierce and bright as a bugle call. He heard her struggling alongside of him.

Suddenly everything changed. Without warning, the black umbrella of the Hobbyhorse slumped and became still.

'Tom? You there?'

'Yes. I think so.'

'You OK?'

'Yes.'

'I . . . uh . . . I think we *killed* it,' said Regan. She pushed up at the stretched fabric that covered the heavy wooden structure of the Hobbyhorse.

Tom got his fingers in under the hooped frame and lifted. Light flooded in. Together, they tipped the inert mass onto its side against the wall. The head cracked off and fell to the floor at Regan's side. It rocked to and fro, its wooden jaw hanging open, its eyes blank and comical.

'Mess with *me*, huh, ya dumb pile of junk!' Regan snarled, whacking the horse across the snout. 'Ow!' She sucked her stinging fingers.

She glanced at Tom. 'It bit me,' she said with a grin.

'Yeah, I saw.'

'Uh . . . were you scared at any stage?'

Tom scratched his nose. 'Nope.'

'No. Me neither,' said Regan. 'I knew we had it licked.' She stood up. Her knees buckled and she found herself on her behind on the carpet again. 'I . . . uh . . . I think I'll just stay here for a minute,' she said casually. 'Hey? You wanna go find a phone?'

Tom stood up and wobbled unsteadily along the corridor. If he was going to collapse, he certainly didn't intend doing it in front of Regan.

He pushed through swing doors into one of the bar rooms. A payphone hung on the wall. He snatched it down and punched out the code for the police.

Regan appeared at his shoulder.

'And don't forget,' she said breathlessly, 'tell 'em the whole darned village has gone totally, utterly and completely *insane!*'

Frankie sprang up and skirted the bonfire, looking for some break in the wall of flames. She could see how the bonfire-stack leaned back into the hillside. Access to the top of the bonfire – where she had seen Jack – would be easier from higher up the hill.

She saw the bridge of planks. It was still intact, shrouded in smoke. She wiped soot-smeared sweat off her forehead. Her whole body ached. The heat beat against her face. She tested the planks with one foot. A brilliant scarf of crimson fire unfurled in her eyes, bursting up between the planks. The heat drove her back.

'*Jack!*' The panic in her own voice startled her.

She heard a heavy, soft sound behind her and something hit her hard in the back. She stumbled forwards with a scream. The flames shrank away from her and the smoke parted like curtains.

She glanced over her shoulder. The pony stood watching her. The wild brown pony. It stamped its fore-hoof and nodded its head, as though urging her on.

She ran forwards through a tunnel of cool air whose walls were formed of smoke and flame. She came to Jack, bound fast to the post. Fire was all around him but the post stood safe in a stomach of still, calm air.

Frankie unwound the ropes that held the wicker frame to the black post. Gently, carefully, she tipped the framework forwards. The wicker fibres loosened from Jack's body, all their power gone. He kicked and fought his way out of the dreadful cage. He tore his gag loose and sucked in a deep breath of clear air.

'It's for real!' he coughed as Frankie helped him to his feet. 'Mr Fox has gone insane. Frankie – they were going to let me burn!'

'I know, I know,' exclaimed Frankie. 'It's all . . . too . . . much . . . to . . . take . . . in.' She filled her lungs. 'Can you walk?'

Jack tested his legs. 'Yes. I think so.'

Frankie grabbed his hand and the two of them ran pell-mell down the smouldering bridge of planks. A fountain of flame blew up behind them and the bridge fell in on itself.

They stumbled and fell, sprawling on the hillside. The fire scorched their clothes. Jack struggled to his knees, pulling Frankie up with him. They ran on a few more metres and then collapsed together in the long grass.

Frankie dragged her straggling hair out of her eyes.

The wind had died down as quickly as it had

come. The bonfire roared, the white smoke pluming and mushrooming up into the clear blue sky.

The pony was gone.

Jack and Frankie looked at one another. Frankie reached out and peeled a sliver of green leaf off Jack's cheek. The faces of both of them were smeared and grimed with soot and sweat.

They heard shouts from lower down the hill.

A small group of people were gathered around something red and yellow that lay like a discarded marionette in the grass near the foot of the bonfire.

A voice rose above the general hubbub.

'Someone fetch a doctor! It's Mr Fox! I think he's had a heart attack!'

CHAPTER SIXTEEN
Blood Sacrifice

'He'll be all right, don't worry.' The green-clad paramedic patted Frankie's shoulder. Frankie rose up on tiptoe and tried to give Jack a final wave as the ambulance doors were closed on him. Jack was lying down. Tom was sitting at his side. Tom saw her and waved back.

'He'll only need a quick check-over at the hospital,' the woman said with a reassuring smile. 'We just need to know that all that smoke didn't do anything nasty to him. His parents will be there for him. He'll probably be back home in a couple of hours.' The smile widened. 'Is he your boyfriend, then?'

'Sorry?' Frankie blinked at her. 'My . . . ? Oh, no. No, no. We're just friends.'

The woman climbed into the ambulance. Although she knew Jack couldn't see her, Frankie still waved as the vehicle headed off down the high street. It seemed like the right thing to do.

She turned to face the police officer.

'OK,' Frankie said tiredly. 'I'm ready now.' The police had made phone calls to everyone's parents.

They got the answerphone at Regan's house. The Christmases were driving straight to the hospital. They had phoned Frankie's home, too. Samantha wouldn't leave the baby. Her dad couldn't be contacted. Samantha said she'd try to get in touch with him; he'd come to collect Frankie and take her home as soon as possible.

'Come and have a sit down in the back of the car,' said the officer. 'We can chat there. You look shattered.'

Frankie attempted to smile. 'I am . . . a bit . . .'

A few people were still hanging about in muttering clusters up and down the grey length of Bodin Summerley's high street. Red and yellow balloons still bobbed and the bunting still looped from house to house, from tree to tree. But the carnival trappings seemed horribly out of place now that the festival had been so tragically halted.

Another ambulance had already left. It had taken Mr Fox away.

The heart attack had been fatal. The old man was dead.

As Frankie and the policewoman headed toward the furthest of the three squad cars, Frankie heard Regan's raised voice.

'Look, I'm telling you, that guy locked us in the pub cellar. Ask Tom. He'll tell you.'

Frankie looked over at the little group. Regan was standing between two police officers. Mr Lovejoy faced her, an innocent, baffled look on his face. He shook his head slowly from side to side and spread his hands out.

'It was just fun and games,' he said. 'Practical jokes are all part of the May Day tradition around here.'

'Yeah! Like heck it was fun and games!' shouted Regan.

Frankie's eyes narrowed in anger and she stormed over to them. She stood in front of Mr Lovejoy and stared up into his face.

'Was it a *game* when you and Miss Tatum threatened me with a knife?' she said. 'Was it all part of the *fun* when you nearly strangled me?'

Mr Lovejoy looked beseechingly at the police officers. 'Well, really,' he said. 'I know these children must be upset, but this is such a gross distortion of the facts.' He smiled at Frankie. 'I'm really very, very sorry that you took it the wrong way, but I can assure you absolutely, with my hand on my heart, that the whole thing was meant in fun.' His plump hand rested on his chest and he looked at the police officers again. 'I sincerely had no idea that these children would take it all so seriously.' He laughed. 'I mean, honestly, do I look the sort of person who'd go around *murdering* my guests? What sort of land-lord would that make me?'

'What about Jack?' said Regan. 'If Frankie hadn't saved him, he would probably have been burned alive!'

Mr Lovejoy lifted his hands to his cheeks. 'I know, I know,' he intoned. 'Don't keep reminding me.' He smiled benevolently at Frankie. 'If not for this young lady's quick thinking, we could have had *two* tragedies on our hands instead of just the one.' He shook his head mournfully. 'Poor Godfrey. He'll be sorely missed. It's a great loss to the village. A terrible loss.'

'Don't listen to him,' said Frankie. 'They were going to burn Jack alive because of that stupid horse's head. They thought some kind of ghost was going to come and do terrible things to them if they didn't provide a couple of human sacrifices.'

'You tell 'em, Frankie!' said Regan. 'Tell 'em about the ghost horse!'

Mr Lovejoy looked at the police officers. 'Now, tell me, seriously: have you ever heard the like?'

'Listen, Miss Fitzgerald, Miss Vanderlinden,' said one of the officers, looking from Frankie to Regan. 'Mr Lovejoy is on the parish council. He's a respected person.' Frankie looked like she was about to explode. 'Listen to me, please,' said the officer. 'I want you to calm down and have a good long think about what you're saying.' He looked at Frankie and his voice became annoyingly patronizing. 'You've had a dreadful shock, seeing Mr Fox ... seeing ... well, you know. Seeing him pass away like that. And, like Mr Lovejoy just said, if not for your presence of mind, your friend ... er ... Jack ... might have been badly burned. All in all, are you *sure* you're thinking straight? Shock can have strange effects, you know. Not just physical effects, either.'

'Jack was tied to a pole in the middle of the bonfire,' Frankie said as evenly as she could manage. 'They were going to let him be burned.' She jabbed a finger at Mr Lovejoy. 'He was in on it. And Miss Tatum. Talk to her, you'll find out! Interrogate her!'

'Florella is in shock,' said Mr Lovejoy. 'It's plain foolishness to accuse her of such things. And as I've been saying for the past hour, Jack would have been released from the bonfire in plenty of time, if poor Godfrey hadn't collapsed the way he did.'

'Jack told me he was behaving crazily,' said Frankie. 'As if he'd gone mad or something.'

'Godfrey was just fine the last time I saw him,' said Mr Lovejoy. 'But if he was behaving a little strangely, is it anything to be wondered at, eh? He's been under a great deal of strain, helping to organize the festival; and then he was attacked in his own home and knocked unconscious.'

'He wasn't attacked,' said Frankie. 'He faked it. He still had the head. I saw it.'

'Yeah,' added Regan. 'And what about all this kooky stuff that's been happening to us over the past few days, huh? How do you explain that?'

'Regan, don't,' said Frankie. They weren't being believed as it was. How would the police react to being told that something supernatural had invaded the village?

But it was too late.

'What kooky stuff?' asked one of the police officers.

Regan planted her hands on her hips. 'Well, for a start,' she said. 'See those trees over there? Well, a couple of days ago we followed a horse in there and we found ourselves in a complete other world! It was really wild, I'm telling you. Like, the trees seemed to go on for ever, and the horse kept appearing and disappearing. And Jack said that Frankie got kind of *possessed*. And then I kept seeing horses everywhere. And then Tom and I got attacked by this Hobby-horse-thing. Except that there was no one in the costume. It was, like, moving about on its own!' Regan paused. 'Uh . . . shouldn't someone be writing all this down?'

The police officers were looking at Regan as though they didn't know whether to burst out laughing or send for a psychiatrist.

'Oh, Regan!' groaned Frankie.

'What?' Regan demanded. 'What? It's all true. Every word of it.'

'I think we're dealing with some over-active imaginations here,' said one of the officers. He frowned at Regan. 'You want to be careful what you tell people,' he said firmly. 'Some people might start to think your stairs don't quite reach your attic. Know what I mean?'

'The nerve of that police guy!' said Regan. 'He was more or less implying that I was crazy!'

'He didn't just *imply* it,' said Frankie. 'He came right out and said it!'

It was two days after the dreadful events of the May Day festival. Regan, Tom, Jack and Frankie were gathered in Darryl Pepper's cluttered attic, seated on some enormous old multi-coloured cushions which Darryl had dragged out of a corner.

Darryl was perched on his chair. Over his shoulder, the computer screensaver poured endless stars towards them. Silhouetted against the late afternoon light, Darryl looked more than ever like an inquisitive stork, with his beaky nose and his unkempt hair standing up like a crest.

The friends had come to him because they had a problem.

'You see,' Frankie said hesitantly, 'some really weird things happened during the festival—'

'And before!' interrupted Regan.

'Yes. And before.' Frankie nodded. 'I've tried and tried to come up with some rational explanation of these things, but I can't.' She paused. 'Er, the thing is, Darryl, in some of the talks you gave to ACE last year, it seemed like you were suggesting that supernatural things might be . . . um . . . real.'

Darryl stared at her but said nothing.

'The local newspaper wrote that Mr Fox was suffering from some kind of nervous breakdown just before he died,' said Jack. 'And I'd go along with that if not for the weird things that were happening to Frankie and Tom and Regan at the same time.' He shook his head. 'And then, like Frankie says, there was the other stuff.'

Over the past two days the four of them had privately talked through all that had happened to them on the First of May. Mr Fox had gone crazy. OK, fine. Mr Lovejoy and Miss Tatum were playing some sort of cruel practical joke. Well, possibly.

But the other things? The Hobbyhorse? The things that Jack had seen whilst being goaded along to beat the village bounds? The wild pony that had led them to that impossible forest – that had attacked them – and that had then helped Frankie to save Jack from the fire? What did it all mean?

Darryl peered thoughtfully at them. 'The way I see it,' he said, 'there are three possible answers.' His eyes gleamed. 'One, you're all playing some silly game.'

'Excuse me!' said Regan. 'I don't *think* so!'

'Two, you were all suffering from hysterics and hallucinations.'

'That's what the police thought,' murmured Tom.

'Three,' Darryl continued. 'Some strange old power woke up in Bodin Summerley, and all the experiences you had were real.' He smiled. 'OK, which option do you prefer?'

There was a long silence.

'Prefer or *believe*?' Jack said at last.

'But if it really was some Celtic god or whatever,' said Tom. 'And if it woke up in a bad mood because the horse-head was dug up, then . . . um – I'm not sure how to put this – is it still around?'

'And is it still after blood?' added Regan.

'Who says it was ever after blood?' said Darryl.

They stared at him.

'It was totally evil,' said Regan. 'What else was going on?'

'I have no idea,' said Darryl. He looked at Frankie. 'What do you think?'

Frankie paused, her eyes lowered. 'It wasn't evil,' she said. 'No. I don't think it was evil.' She looked up. 'It was angry, that's for sure. But it helped us in the end.' She looked at Darryl. 'But what was it? A goody or a baddy?'

'Neither,' said Darryl. 'It was just a force of nature – of supernature, if you like. An elemental force – like the wind. Except that it has a mind. But you shouldn't think of it as bad or good. It isn't either.'

'So, what did it want?' Jack asked. 'What was going on?'

'I think it woke up angry when the head was disinterred,' said Darryl. He shrugged. 'Maybe it's a bad idea to try and take back gifts of that sort – gifts freely given to ancient powers. Maybe they take it as a sign of disrespect if people come along and dig 'em up again.' He looked at them, his eyes glittering behind his glasses. 'And maybe everything was put right when the head fell into the bonfire. Maybe burning it did the trick. Or, if it wasn't that, maybe it did get its blood sacrifice after all. Of sorts.'

'Mr Fox!' gasped Frankie. 'Yes. Everything seemed different after Mr Fox went down. The pony helped me rescue Jack.'

'And that was about the same time that the Hobby-horse collapsed,' said Tom. 'Creepy!'

'Everything calmed down then,' said Jack. 'It was

as if all that . . . all that power just went back to sleep again.'

'Uh, Darryl?' asked Regan. 'One question. Do you think Lovejoy and the other guys really meant to kill Frankie and Jack? I mean, *really*?'

'I'm sure the festival was just meant to be a jolly day out when they set it up,' Darryl said. 'The fact that the head was dug up at the same time was just a coincidence.' He frowned. 'If you believe in coincidences like that, of course.' He shook his head. 'Still, it's pretty clear that Mr Fox and the landlord and old Miss Tatum were overwhelmed by the power that was aroused when the head hit the air. I think they lost themselves in their own ancestral past.' He smiled bleakly. 'They must have believed they were born-again druids. For a while, anyway – until Godfrey Fox keeled over. I think that snapped the other two out of it. I think he was their leader.' There was a pause. 'And, yes,' Darryl said. 'Yes, I do think that they meant to kill Frankie and Jack.'

Regan looked at her friends. 'Now that,' she said dramatically, 'is what I call totally creepy. Creepy to the *max*!'

There was a long silence while they all reflected on the thought of jolly Mr Lovejoy and gentle Miss Tatum still living their quiet lives only a few miles away.

'I think I'll steer clear of that place in future,' Regan said at last. 'Nuts! I just wish we had some way of convincing people about the stuff that was going down back there.'

'Listen,' said Frankie, 'I've been thinking.' She looked around at her friends. 'We all know what really happened in Bodin Summerley. The super-natural things, I mean. But we're never ever going

147

to be able to convince other people. We don't have any proof. And it's all too weird. For heaven's sake, I wouldn't believe it if I hadn't been there. So, why worry about convincing other people? *We* know what happened – why should we care what other people think?'

'That sounds like a sensible option,' said Darryl. 'You don't want people thinking you're odd. Because, if you stick to your story, that's what will happen. Believe me.'

They looked at him. Potty Pepper. Regan opened her mouth, but closed it again without speaking.

'If you feel the need to talk about those things,' said Darryl, 'you're welcome to come up here to do it. I won't think you're odd.'

'Thanks,' said Jack. 'I think we just might take you up on that.'

'There's still one problem,' said Tom. 'The project for Tinkerbell.'

'For who?' said Darryl. 'Oh, you mean Carol Tinker. I'd never thought of calling her that.' He laughed. 'But it suits her. Nice one, Tom.'

'What about the project, Tom?' asked Jack.

'Well, she wanted us to write down everything we could find out about May Day festivals, right?' said Tom. 'So, do we include all the freaky stuff that happened to us, or not?'

'No, we don't,' said Frankie. 'Mrs Tinker would throw a fit. She'd think we weren't taking it seriously. We'd probably get slung out of the club.'

'So,' said Jack. 'We keep it to ourselves, right? Just the four of us.'

'*Five* of us, I think,' said Darryl with a wide grin. 'Someone needs to keep a record of what really happened in Bodin Summerley.' He spun to face his computer. He tapped at the keyboard and a blank screen appeared.

'Now then,' he said. 'I think we'll call this file *The Wicker Man*.' He looked at them over his shoulder. 'OK, people, I want you to tell me the whole story all over again. And don't miss anything out.'

Afterword

Throughout the British Isles, people still celebrate the arrival of May Day with a whole array of different traditional activities – but few realize the bloodthirsty history that lurks behind these apparently harmless festivities.

Julius Caesar was one of the first authorities to write about the human sacrifices practised by the Druid priests of the Celtic peoples of Europe and Great Britain. He told of bloodstained groves, of riotous feasting and dancing and of ritual fires lit at the turning points of the year.

At these times, giant wickerwork frames were constructed and filled with sacrificial offerings: both human and animal. These wicker giants were then burned with the living victims still inside. It seemed, in those days, that a lot of blood was needed to keep the wheels of the world turning.

Beltane – May Day – was one of the most important of all the pagan festivals, and many ancient May Day rites have lasted down the centuries. 'Fun' versions of them are still played out to this day.

On Walpurgis Night – the Eve of May Day – people still pretend to drive 'evil spirits' away by taking to the street with lighted torches: shouting, singing, beating drums and dancing. On this night, all fires in the area are extinguished.

Human sacrifices – especially children – were preferred for the May Day rites. A local girl would be elected as May Queen and a boy picked to be the May King, also known as the Green Man, Green Georgie or Jack-in-the-Green. Both would be symbolically sacrificed at the end of the day's celebrations: the boy on the Beltane bonfire, and the girl, tied to a tree in a sacred grove, stabbed to death with a ritual knife.

The point of this ritual slaughter was to release the spirits of the sacrifices from the physical limitations of the human body, and to allow them to be reincarnated and revitalized to spread life-giving power throughout the land.

Of course, these days, the sacrifices are only symbolic – the May Queen and May King are just a colourful part of the fun and games of a modern May Day parade. No one is actually killed. Usually.

Allan Frewin Jones
Dark Paths 2:
THE PLAGUE PIT

Tom is sick with fear. Literally.

The hospital has done all the tests, but they don't know what's wrong. Of course, being accidentally buried under a putrid avalanche of stinking human remains was blatantly not good for him. But the doctors will soon sort him out, right?

Wrong. Badly wrong. Tom's brother Jack knows that their excavations have put him in terrible danger. The evil of the old days is all around them. The rats are running – and even modern medicine cannot save Tom from the bubonic plague . . .

Books in the DARK PATHS series available from Macmillan

The prices shown below are correct at the time of going to press. However, Macmillan Publishers reserve the right to show new retail prices on covers which may differ from those previously advertised.

ALLAN FREWIN JONES

1. The Wicker Man		0 330 36806 0	£3.99
2. The Plague Pit		0 330 36807 9	£3.99
3. Unquiet Graves	*Jan. 1999*	0 330 36808 7	£3.99
4. The Phantom Airman	*Mar. 1999*	0 330 36809 5	£3.99
5. The Wreckers	*May 1999*	0 330 36810 9	£3.99
6. The Monk's Curse	*July 1999*	0 330 36811 7	£3.99

All Macmillan titles can be ordered at your local bookshop or are available by post from:

Book Service by Post
PO Box 29, Douglas, Isle of Man IM99 1BQ

Credit cards accepted. For details:
Telephone: 01624 675137
Fax: 01624 670923
E-mail: bookshop@enterprise.net

Free postage and packing in the UK.
Overseas customers: add £1 per book (paperback)
and £3 per book (hardback).